CW00688194

A MASTER OF MYSTERIES

A MASTER OF MYSTERIES

L. T. MEADE AND ROBERT EUSTACE

WILDSIDE PRESS

Published by Wildside Press LLC.
www.wildsidebooks.com

CONTENTS

INTRODUCTION

It so happened that the circumstances of fate allowed me to follow my own bent in the choice of a profession. From my earliest youth the weird, the mysterious had an irresistible fascination for me. Having private means, I resolved to follow my unique inclinations, and I am now well known to all my friends as a professional exposer of ghosts, and one who can clear away the mysteries of most haunted houses. Up to the present I have never had cause to regret my choice, but at the same time I cannot too strongly advise any one who thinks of following my example to hesitate before engaging himself in tasks that entail time, expense, thankless labour, often ridicule, and not seldom great personal danger. To explain, by the application of science, phenomena attributed to spiritual agencies has been the work of my life. I have, naturally, gone through strange difficulties in accomplishing my mission. I propose in these pages to relate the histories of certain queer events, enveloped at first in mystery, and apparently dark with portent, but, nevertheless, when grappled with in the true spirit of science, capable of explanation.

THE MYSTERY OF THE CIRCULAR CHAMBER

One day in late September I received the following letter from my lawyer:— —

"My Dear Bell,—

"I shall esteem it a favour if you can make it convenient to call upon me at ten o'clock to-morrow morning on a matter of extreme privacy."

At the appointed hour I was shown into Mr. Edgcombe's private room. I had known him for years—we were, in fact, old friends—and I was startled now by the look of worry, not to say anxiety, on his usually serene features.

"You are the very man I want, Bell," he cried. "Sit down; I have a great deal to say to you. There is a mystery of a very grave nature which I hope you may solve for me. It is in connection with a house said to be haunted."

He fixed his bright eyes on my face as he spoke. I sat perfectly silent, waiting for him to continue.

"In the first place," he resumed, "I must ask you to regard the matter as confidential."

"Certainly," I answered.

"You know," he went on, "that I have often laughed at your special hobby, but it occurred to me yesterday that the experiences you have lived through may enable you to give me valuable assistance in this difficulty."

"I will do my best for you, Edgcombe," I replied.

He lay back in his chair, folding his hands.

"The case is briefly as follows," he began. "It is connected with the family of the Wentworths. The only son, Archibald, the artist, has just died under most extraordinary circumstances. He was, as you probably know, one of the most promising water-colour painters of the younger school, and his pictures in this year's Academy met with universal praise. He was the heir to the Wentworth estates, and his death has caused a complication of claims from a member of a collateral branch of the family, who, when the present squire dies, is entitled to the money. This man has spent the greater part of his life in Australia, is badly off, and evidently belongs to a rowdy set. He has been to see me two or three times, and I must say frankly that I am not taken with his appearance."

"Had he anything to do with the death?" I interrupted.

"Nothing whatever, as you will quickly perceive. Wentworth has been accustomed from time to time to go alone on sketching tours to different parts of the country. He has tramped about on foot, and visited odd, out-of-the-way nooks searching for subjects. He never took much money with him, and always travelled as an apparently poor man. A month ago he started off alone on one of these tours. He had a handsome commission from Barlow & Co., picture-dealers in the Strand. He was to paint certain parts of the river Merran; and although he certainly did not need money, he seemed glad of an object for a good ramble. He parted with his family in the best of health and spirits, and wrote to them from time to time; but a week ago they heard the news that he had died suddenly at an inn on the Merran. There was, of course, an inquest and an autopsy. Dr. Miles Gordon, the Wentworths' consulting physician, was telegraphed for, and was present at the post-mortem examination. He is absolutely puzzled to account for the death. The medical examination showed Wentworth to be in apparently perfect health at the time. There was no lesion to be discovered upon which to base a different opinion, all the organs being healthy. Neither was there any trace of poison, nor marks of violence. The coroner's verdict was that Wentworth died of syncope, which, as you know perhaps, is a synonym for an unknown cause. The inn where he died is a very lonely one, and has the reputation of being haunted. The landlord seems to bear a bad character, although nothing has ever been proved against him. But a young girl who lives at the inn gave evidence which at first startled every one. She said at the inquest that she had earnestly warned Wentworth not to sleep in the haunted room. She had scarcely told the coroner so before she fell to the floor in an epileptic fit. When she came to herself she was sullen and silent, and nothing more could be extracted from her. The old man, the innkeeper, explained that the girl was half-witted, but he did not attempt to deny that the house had the reputation of being haunted, and said that he had himself begged Wentworth not to put up there. Well, that is about the whole of the story. The coroner's inquest seems to deny the evidence of foul play, but I have my very strong suspicions. What I want you to do is to ascertain if they are correct. Will you undertake the case?"

"I will certainly do so," I replied. "Please let me have any further particulars, and a written document to show, in case of need, that I am acting under your directions."

Edgcombe agreed to this, and I soon afterwards took my leave. The case had the features of an interesting problem, and I hoped that I should prove successful in solving it.

That evening I made my plans carefully. I would go into ——shire early on the following morning, assuming for my purpose the character of an amateur photographer. Having got all necessary particulars from Edgcombe, I made a careful mental map of my operations. First of all I would visit a little village of the name of Harkhurst, and put up at the inn, the Crown and Thistle. Here Wentworth had spent a fortnight when he first started on his commission to make drawings of the river Merran. I thought it likely that I should obtain some information there. Circumstances must guide me as to my further steps, but my intention was to proceed from Harkhurst to the Castle Inn, which was situated about six miles further up the river. This was the inn where the tragedy had occurred.

Towards evening on the following day I arrived at Harkhurst. When my carriage drew up at the Crown and

Thistle, the landlady was standing in the doorway. She was a buxom-looking dame, with a kindly face. I asked for a bed.

"Certainly, sir," she answered. She turned with me into the little inn, and taking me upstairs, showed me a small room, quite clean and comfortable, looking out on the yard. I said it would do capitally, and she hurried downstairs to prepare my supper. After this meal, which proved to be excellent, I determined to visit the landlord in the bar. I found him chatty and communicative.

"This is a lonely place," he said; "we don't often have a soul staying with us for a month at a time." As he spoke he walked to the door, and I followed him. The shades of night were beginning to fall, but the picturesqueness of the little hamlet could not but commend itself to me.

"And yet it is a lovely spot," I said. "I should have thought tourists would have thronged to it. It is at least an ideal place for photographers."

"You are right there, sir," replied the man; "and although we don't often have company to stay in the inn, now and then we have a stray artist. It's not three weeks back," he continued, "that we had a gentleman like you, sir, only a bit younger, to stay with us for a week or two. He was an artist, and drew from morning till night—ah, poor fellow!"

"Why do you say that?" I asked.

"I have good cause, sir. Here, wife," continued the landlord, looking over his shoulder at Mrs. Johnson, the landlady, who now appeared on the scene, "this gentleman has been asking me questions about our visitor, Mr. Wentworth, but perhaps we ought not to inflict such a dismal story upon him to-night."

"Pray do," I said; "what you have already hinted at arouses my curiosity. Why should you pity Mr. Wentworth?"

"He is dead, sir," said the landlady, in a solemn voice. I gave a pretended start, and she continued,—

"And it was all his own fault. Ah, dear! it makes me almost cry to think of it. He was as nice a gentleman as I ever set eyes on, and so strong, hearty, and pleasant. Well, sir, everything went well until one day he said to me, 'I am about to leave you, Mrs. Johnson. I am going to a little place called the Castle Inn, further up the Merran.'

"'The Castle Inn!' I cried. 'No, Mr. Wentworth, that you won't, not if you value your life.'

"'And why not?' he said, looking at me with as merry blue eyes as you ever saw in anybody's head. 'Why should I not visit the Castle Inn? I have a commission to make some drawings of that special bend of the river.'

"'Well, then, sir,' I answered, 'if that is the case, you'll just have a horse and trap from here and drive over as often as you want to. For the Castle Inn ain't a fit place for a Christian to put up at.'

"'What do you mean?' he asked of me.

"'It is said to be haunted, sir, and what does happen in that house the Lord only knows, but there's not been a visitor at the inn for some years, not since Bailiff Holt came by his death.'

"'Came by his death?' he asked. 'And how was that?'

"'God knows, but I don't,' I answered. 'At the coroner's inquest it was said that he died from syncope, whatever that means, but the folks round here said it was fright.' Mr. Wentworth just laughed at me. He didn't mind a word I said, and the next day, sir, he was off, carrying his belongings with him."

"Well, and what happened?" I asked, seeing that she paused.

"What happened, sir? Just what I expected. Two days afterwards came the news of his death. Poor young gentleman! He died in the very room where Holt had breathed his last; and, oh, if there wasn't a fuss and to-do, for it turned out that, although he seemed quite poor to us, with little or no money, he was no end of a swell, and had rich relations, and big estates coming to him; and, of course, there was a coroner's inquest and all the rest, and great doctors came down from London, and our Dr. Stanmore, who lives down the street, was sent for, and though they did all they could, and examined him, as it were, with a microscope, they could find no cause for death, and so they give it out that it was syncope, just as they did in the case of poor Holt. But, sir, it wasn't; it was fright, sheer fright. The place is haunted. It's a mysterious, dreadful house, and I only hope you won't have nothing to do with it."

She added a few more words and presently left us.

"That's a strange story," I said, turning to Johnson; "your wife has excited my curiosity. I should much like to get further particulars."

"There don't seem to be anything more to tell, sir," replied Johnson. "It's true what the wife says, that the Castle Inn has a bad name. It's not the first, no, nor the second, death that has occurred there."

"You mentioned your village doctor; do you think he could enlighten me on the subject?"

"I am sure he would do his best, sir. He lives only six doors away, in a red house. Maybe you wouldn't mind stepping down the street and speaking to him?"

"You are sure he would not think it a liberty?"

"Not he, sir; he'll be only too pleased to exchange a word with some one outside this sleepy little place."

"Then I'll call on him," I answered, and taking up my hat I strolled down the street. I was lucky in finding Dr. Stanmore at home, and the moment I saw his face I determined to take him into my confidence.

"The fact is this," I said, when he had shaken hands with me, "I should not dream of taking this liberty did I not feel certain that you could help me."

"And in what way?" he asked, not stiffly, but with a keen, inquiring, interested glance.

"I have been sent down from London to inquire into the Wentworth mystery," I said.

"Is that so?" he said, with a start. Then he continued gravely: "I fear you have come on a wild-goose chase. There was nothing discovered at the autopsy to account for the death. There were no marks on the body, and all the organs were healthy. I met Wentworth often while he was staying here, and he was as hearty and strong-looking a young man as I have ever come across."

"But the Castle Inn has a bad reputation," I said.

"That is true; the people here are afraid of it. It is said to be haunted. But really, sir, you and I need not trouble ourselves about stupid reports of that sort. Old Bindloss, the landlord, has lived there for years, and there has never been anything proved against him."

"Is he alone?"

"No; his wife and a grandchild live there also."

"A grandchild?" I said. "Did not this girl give some startling evidence at the inquest?"

"Nothing of any consequence," replied Dr. Stanmore; "she only repeated what Bindloss had already said himself—that the house was haunted, and that she had asked Wentworth not to sleep in the room."

"Has anything ever been done to explain the reason why this room is said to be haunted?" I continued.

"Not that I know of. Rats are probably at the bottom of it."

"But have not there been other deaths in the house?"

"That is true."

"How many?"

"Well, I have myself attended no less than three similar inquests."

"And what was the verdict of the jury?"

"In each case the verdict was death from syncope."

"Which means, cause unknown," I said, jumping impatiently to my feet. "I wonder, Dr. Stanmore, that you are satisfied to leave the matter in such a state."

"And, pray, what can I do?" he inquired. "I am asked to examine a body. I find all the organs in perfect health; I cannot trace the least appearance of violence, nor can I detect poison. What other evidence can I honestly give?"

"I can only say that I should not be satisfied," I replied. "I now wish to add that I have come down from London determined to solve this mystery. I shall myself put up at the Castle Inn."

"Well?" said Dr. Stanmore.

"And sleep in the haunted room."

"Of course you don't believe in the ghost."

"No; but I believe in foul play. Now, Dr. Stanmore, will you help me?"

"Most certainly, if I can. What do you wish me to do?"

"This—I shall go to the Castle Inn to-morrow. If at the end of three days I do not return here, will you go in search of me, and at the same time post this letter to Mr. Edgcombe, my London lawyer?"

"If you do not appear in three days I'll kick up no end of a row," said Dr. Stanmore, "and, of course, post your letter."

Soon afterwards I shook hands with the doctor and left him.

After an early dinner on the following day, I parted with my good-natured landlord and his wife, and with my knapsack and kodak strapped over my shoulders, started on my way. I took care to tell no one that I was going to the Castle Inn, and for this purpose doubled back through a wood, and so found the right road. The sun was nearly setting when at last I approached a broken-down signpost, on which, in half-obliterated characters, I could read the words, "To the Castle Inn." I found myself now at the entrance of a small lane, which was evidently little frequented, as it was considerably grass-grown. From where I stood I could catch no sight of any habitation, but just at that moment a low, somewhat inconsequent laugh fell upon my ears. I turned quickly and saw a pretty girl, with bright eyes and a childish face, gazing at me with interest. I had little doubt that she was old Bindloss's grand-daughter.

"Will you kindly tell me," I asked, "if this is the way to the Castle Inn?"

My remark evidently startled her. She made a bound forward, seized me by my hand, and tried to push me away from the entrance to the lane into the high road.

"Go away!" she cried; "we have no beds fit for gentlemen at the Castle Inn. Go! go!" she continued, and she pointed up the winding road. Her eyes were now blazing in her head, but I noticed that her lips trembled, and that very little would cause her to burst into tears.

"But I am tired and footsore," I answered. "I should like to put up at the inn for the night."

"Don't!" she repeated; "they'll put you into a room with a ghost. Don't go; 'tain't a place for gentlemen." Here she burst not into tears, but into a fit of high, shrill, almost idiotic laughter. She suddenly clapped one of her hands to her forehead, and, turning, flew almost as fast as the wind down the narrow lane and out of sight.

I followed her quickly. I did not believe that the girl was quite as mad as she seemed, but I had little doubt that she had something extraordinary weighing on her mind.

At the next turn I came in view of the inn. It was a queer-looking old place, and I stopped for a moment to look at it.

The house was entirely built of stone. There were two storeys to the centre part, which was square, and at the four corners stood four round towers. The house was built right on the river, just below a large mill-pond. I walked up to the door and pounded on it with my stick. It was shut, and looked as inhospitable as the rest of the place. After a moment's delay it was opened two or three inches, and the surly face of an old woman peeped out.

"And what may you be wanting?" she asked.

"A bed for the night," I replied; "can you accommodate me?"

She glanced suspiciously first at me and then at my camera.

"You are an artist, I make no doubt," she said, "and we don't want no more of them here."

She was about to slam the door in my face, but I pushed my foot between it and the lintel.

"I am easily pleased," I said; "can you not give me some sort of bed for the night?"

"You had best have nothing to do with us," she answered. "You go off to Harkhurst; they can put you up at the Crown and Thistle."

"I have just come from there," I answered. "As a matter of fact, I could not walk another mile."

"We don't want visitors at the Castle Inn," she continued. Here she peered forward and looked into my face. "You had best be off," she repeated; "they say the place is haunted."

I uttered a laugh.

"You don't expect me to believe that?" I said. She glanced at me from head to foot. Her face was ominously grave.

"You had best know all, sir," she said, after a pause. "Something happens in this house, and no living soul knows what it is, for they who have seen it have never yet survived to tell the tale. It's not more than a week back that a young gentleman came here. He was like you, bold as brass, and he too wanted a bed, and would take no denial. I told him plain, and so did my man, that the place was haunted. He didn't mind no more than you mind. Well, he slept in the only room we have got for guests, and he—he *died there*."

"What did he die of?" I asked.

"Fright," was the answer, brief and laconic. "Now do you want to come or not?"

"Yes; I don't believe in ghosts. I want the bed, and I am determined to have it."

The woman flung the door wide open.

"Don't say as I ain't warned you," she cried. "Come in, if you must." She led me into the kitchen, where a fire burned sullenly on the hearth.

"Sit you down, and I'll send for Bindloss," she said. "I can only promise to give you a bed if Bindloss agrees. Liz, come along here this minute."

A quick young step was heard in the passage, and the pretty girl whom I had seen at the top of the lane entered. Her eyes sought my face, her lips moved as if to say something, but no sound issued from them.

"Go and find your grandad," said the old woman. "Tell him there is a gentleman here that wants a bed. Ask him what's to be done."

The girl favoured me with a long and peculiar glance, then turning on her heel she left the room. As soon as she did so the old woman peered forward and looked curiously at me.

"I'm sorry you are staying," she said; "don't forget as I warned you. Remember, this ain't a proper inn at all. Once it was a mill, but that was afore Bindloss's day and mine. Gents would come in the summer and put up for the fishing, but then the story of the ghost got abroad, and lately we have no visitors to speak of, only an odd one now and then who ain't wanted—no, he ain't wanted. You see, there was three deaths here. Yes"—she held up one of her skinny hands and began to count on her fingers—"yes, three up to the present; three, that's it. Ah, here comes Bindloss."

A shuffling step was heard in the passage, and an old man, bent with age, and wearing a long white beard, entered the room.

"We has no beds for strangers," he said, speaking in an aggressive and loud tone. "Hasn't the wife said so? We don't let out beds here."

"As that is the case, you have no right to have that signpost at the end of the lane," I retorted. "I am not in a mood to walk eight miles for a shelter in a country I know nothing about. Cannot you put me up somehow?"

"I have told the gentleman everything, Sam," said the wife. "He is just for all the world like young Mr. Wentworth, and not a bit frightened."

The old landlord came up and faced me.

"Look you here," he said, "you stay on at your peril. I don't want you, nor do the wife. Now is it 'yes' or 'no'?"

"It is 'yes,'" I said.

"There's only one room you can sleep in."

"One room is sufficient."

"It's the one Mr. Wentworth died in. Hadn't you best take up your traps and be off?"

"No, I shall stay."

"Then there's no more to be said."

"Run, Liz," said the woman, "and light the fire in the parlour."

The girl left the room, and the woman, taking up a candle, said she would take me to the chamber where I was to sleep. She led me down a long and narrow passage, and then, opening a door, down two steps into the most extraordinary-looking room I had ever seen. The walls were completely circular, covered with a paper of a staring grotesque pattern. A small iron bedstead projected into the middle of the floor, which was uncarpeted except for a slip of matting beside it. A cheap deal wash-hand-stand, a couple of chairs, and a small table with a blurred looking-glass stood against the wall beneath a deep embrasure, in which there was a window. This was evidently a room in one of the circular towers. I had never seen less inviting quarters.

"Your supper will be ready directly, sir," said the woman, and placing the candle on the little table, she left me.

The place felt damp and draughty, and the flame of the candle flickered about, causing the tallow to gutter to one side. There was no fireplace in the room, and above, the walls converged to a point, giving the whole place the appearance of an enormous extinguisher. I made a hurried and necessarily limited toilet, and went into the parlour. I was standing by the fire, which was burning badly, when the door opened, and the girl Liz came in, bearing a tray in her hand. She laid the tray on the table and came up softly to me.

"Fools come to this house," she said, "and you are one."

"Pray let me have my supper, and don't talk," I replied. "I am tired and hungry, and want to go to bed."

Liz stood perfectly still for a moment.

"'Tain't worth it," she said; then, in a meditative voice, "no, 'tain't worth it. But I'll say no more. Folks will never be warned!"

Her grandmother's voice calling her caused her to bound from the room.

My supper proved better than I had expected, and, having finished it, I strolled into the kitchen, anxious to have a further talk with the old man. He was seated alone by the fire, a great mastiff lying at his feet.

"Can you tell me why the house is supposed to be haunted?" I asked suddenly, stooping down to speak to him.

"How should I know?" he cried hoarsely. "The wife and me have been here twenty years, and never seen nor heard anything, but for certain folks *do* die in the house. It's mortal unpleasant for me, for the doctors come along, and the coroner, and there's an inquest and no end of fuss. The folks die, although no one has ever laid a finger on 'em; the doctors can't prove why they are dead, but dead they be. Well, there ain't no use saying more. You are here, and maybe you'll pass the one night all right."

"I shall go to bed at once," I said, "but I should like some candles. Can you supply me?"

The man turned and looked at his wife, who at that moment entered the kitchen. She went to the dresser, opened a wooden box, and taking out three or four tallow candles, put them into my hand.

I rose, simulating a yawn.

"Good-night, sir," said the old man; "good-night; I wish you well."

A moment later I had entered my bedroom, and having shut the door, proceeded to give it a careful examination. As far as I could make out, there was no entrance to the room except by the door, which was shaped to fit the circular walls. I noticed, however, that there was an unaccountable draught, and this I at last discovered came from below the oak wainscoting of the wall. I could not in any way account for the draught, but it existed to an unpleasant extent. The bed, I further saw, was somewhat peculiar; it had no castors on the four legs, which were let down about half an inch into sockets provided for them in the wooden floor. This discovery excited my suspicions still further. It was evident that the bed was intended to remain in a particular position. I saw that it directly faced the little window sunk deep into the thick wall, so that any one in bed would look directly at the window. I examined my watch, found that it was past eleven, and placing both the candles on a tiny table near the bed, I lay down without undressing. I was on the alert to catch the slightest noise, but the hours dragged on and nothing occurred. In the house all was silence, and outside the splashing and churning of the water falling over the wheel came distinctly to my ears.

I lay awake all night, but as morning dawned fell into an uneasy sleep. I awoke to see the broad daylight streaming in at the small window.

Making a hasty toilet, I went out for a walk, and presently came in to breakfast. It had been laid for me in the big kitchen, and the old man was seated by the hearth.

"Well," said the woman, "I hope you slept comfortable, sir."

I answered in the affirmative, and now perceived that old Bindloss and his wife were in the humour to be agreeable. They said that if I was satisfied with the room I might spend another night at the inn. I told them that I had a great many photographs to take, and would be much obliged for the permission. As I spoke I looked round for the girl, Liz. She was nowhere to be seen.

"Where is your grand-daughter?" I asked of the old woman.

"She has gone away for the day," was the reply. "It's too much for Liz to see strangers. She gets excited, and then the fits come on."

"What sort of fits?"

"I can't tell what they are called, but they're bad, and weaken her, poor thing! Liz ought never to be excited." Here Bindloss gave his wife a warning glance; she lowered her eyes, and going across to the range, began to stir the contents of something in a saucepan.

That afternoon I borrowed some lines from Bindloss, and, taking an old boat which was moored to the bank of the mill-pond, set off under the pretence of fishing for pike. The weather was perfect for the time of year.

Waiting my opportunity, I brought the boat up to land on the bank that dammed up the stream, and getting out walked along it in the direction of the mill-wheel, over which the water was now rushing.

As I observed it from this side of the bank, I saw that the tower in which my room was placed must at one time have been part of the mill itself, and I further noticed that the masonry was comparatively new, showing that alterations must have taken place when the house was abandoned as a mill and was turned into an inn. I clambered down the side of the wheel, holding on to the beams, which were green and slippery, and peered through the paddles.

As I was making my examination, a voice suddenly startled me.

"What are you doing down there?"

I looked up; old Bindloss was standing on the bank looking down at me. He was alone, and his face was contorted with a queer mixture of fear and passion. I hastily hoisted myself up, and stood beside him.

"What are you poking about down there for?" he said, pushing his ugly old face into mine as he spoke. "You fool! if you had fallen you would have been drowned. No one could swim a stroke in that mill-race. And then there would have been another death, and all the old fuss over again! Look here, sir, will you have the goodness to get out of the place? I don't want you here any more."

"I intend to leave to-morrow morning," I answered in a pacifying voice, "and I am really very much obliged to you for warning me about the mill."

"You had best not go near it again," he said in a menacing voice, and then he turned hastily away. I watched him as he climbed up a steep bank and disappeared from view. He was going in the opposite direction from the house. Seizing the opportunity of his absence, I once more approached the mill. Was it possible that Wentworth had been hurled into it? But had this been the case there would have been signs and marks on the body. Having reached the wheel, I clambered boldly down. It was now getting dusk, but I could see that a prolongation of the axle entered the wall of the tower. The fittings were also in wonderfully good order, and the bolt that held the great wheel only required to be drawn out to set it in motion.

That evening during supper I thought very hard. I perceived that Bindloss was angry, also that he was suspicious and alarmed. I saw plainly that the only way to really discover what had been done to Wentworth was to cause the old ruffian to try similar means to get rid of me. This was a dangerous expedient, but I felt desperate, and my curiosity as well as interest were keenly aroused. Having finished my supper, I went into the passage preparatory to going into the kitchen. I had on felt slippers, and my footfall made no noise. As I approached the door I heard Bindloss saying to his wife,—

"He's been poking about the mill-wheel; I wish he would make himself scarce."

"Oh, he can't find out anything," was the reply. "You keep quiet, Bindloss; he'll be off in the morning."

"That's as maybe," was the answer, and then there came a harsh and very disagreeable laugh. I waited for a moment, and then entered the kitchen. Bindloss was alone now; he was bending over the fire, smoking.

"I shall leave early in the morning," I said, "so please have my bill ready for me." I then seated myself near him, drawing up my chair close to the blaze. He looked as if he resented this, but said nothing.

"I am very curious about the deaths which occur in this house," I said, after a pause. "How many did you say there were?"

"That is nothing to you," he answered. "We never wanted you here; you can go when you please."

"I shall go tomorrow morning, but I wish to say something now."

"And what may that be?"

"I don't believe in that story about the place being haunted."

"Oh, you don't, don't you?" He dropped his pipe, and his glittering eyes gazed at me with a mixture of anger and ill-concealed alarm.

"No," I paused, then I said slowly and emphatically, "I went back to the mill even after your warning, and——"

"What?" he cried, starting to his feet.

"Nothing," I answered; "only I don't believe in the ghost."

His face turned not only white but livid. I left him without another word. I saw that his suspicions had been much strengthened by my words. This I intended. To induce the ruffian to do his worst was the only way to wring his secret from him.

My hideous room looked exactly as it had done on the previous evening. The grotesque pattern on the walls seemed to start out in bold relief. Some of the ugly lines seemed at that moment, to my imagination, almost to take human shape, to convert themselves into ogre-like faces, and to grin at me. Was I too daring? Was it wrong of me to risk my life in this manner? I was terribly tired, and, curious as it may seem, my greatest fear at that crucial moment was the dread that I might fall asleep. I had spent two nights with scarcely any repose, and felt that at any moment, notwithstanding all my efforts, slumber might visit me. In order to give Bindloss full opportunity for carrying out his scheme, it was necessary for me to get into bed, and even to feign sleep. In my present exhausted condition the pretence of slumber would easily lapse into the reality. This risk, however, which really was a very grave one, must be run. Without undressing I got into bed, pulling the bed-clothes well over me. In my hand I held my revolver. I deliberately put out the candles, and then lay motionless, waiting for events. The house was quiet as the grave—there was not a stir, and gradually my nerves, excited as they were, began to calm down. As I had fully expected, overpowering sleepiness seized me, and, notwithstanding every effort, I found myself drifting away into the land of dreams. I began to wish that whatever apparition was to appear would do so at once and get it over. Gradually but surely I seemed to pass from all memory of my present world, and to live in a strange and terrible phantasmagoria. In that state I slept, in that state also I dreamt, and dreamt horribly.

I thought that I was dancing a waltz with an enormously tall woman. She towered above me, clasping me in her arms, and began to whirl me round and round at a giddy speed. I could hear the crashing music of a distant band. Faster and faster, round and round some great empty hall was I whirled. I knew that I was losing my senses, and screamed to her to stop and let me go. Suddenly there was a terrible crash close to me. Good God! I found myself awake, but—I was still moving. Where was I? Where was I going? I leapt up on the bed, only to reel and fall heavily backwards upon the floor. What was the matter? Why was I sliding, sliding? Had I sud-denly gone mad, or was I still suffering from some hideous nightmare? I tried to move, to stagger to my feet. Then by slow degrees my senses began to return, and I knew where I was. I was in the circular room, the room where Wentworth had died; but what was happening to me I could not divine. I only knew that I was being whirled round and round at a velocity that was every moment increasing. By the moonlight that struggled in through the window I saw that the floor and the bed upon it was revolving, but the table was lying on its side, and its fall must have awakened me.

I could not see any other furniture in the room. By what mysterious manner had it been removed? Making a great effort, I crawled to the centre of this awful chamber, and, seizing the foot of the bed, struggled to my feet. Here I knew there would be less motion, and I could just manage to see the outline of the door. I had taken the precaution to slip the revolver into my pocket, and I still felt that if human agency appeared, I had a chance of selling my life dearly; but surely the horror I was passing through was invented by no living man! As the floor of the room revolved in the direction of the door I made a dash for it, but was carried swiftly past, and again fell heavily. When I came round again I made a frantic effort to cling to one of the steps, but in vain; the head of the bedstead caught me as it flew round, and tore my arms away. In another moment I believe I should have gone raving mad with terror. My head felt as if it would burst; I found it impossible to think consecutively. The only idea which really possessed me was a mad wish to escape from this hideous place. I struggled to the bedstead, and dragging the legs from their sockets, pulled it into the middle of the room away from the wall. With this out of the way, I managed at last to reach the door in safety.

The moment my hand grasped the handle I leapt upon the little step and tried to wrench the door open. It was locked, locked from without; it defied my every effort. I had only just standing room for my feet. Below me the floor of the room was still racing round with terrible speed. I dared scarcely look at it, for the giddiness in my head increased each moment. The next instant a soft footstep was distinctly audible, and I saw a gleam of light through a chink of the door. I heard a hand fumbling at the lock, the door was slowly opened outwards, and I saw the face of Bindloss.

For a moment he did not perceive me, for I was crouching down on the step, and the next instant with all my force I flung myself upon him. He uttered a yell of terror. The lantern he carried dropped and went out, but I had gripped him round the neck with my fingers, driving them deep down into his lean, sinewy throat. With frantic speed I pulled him along the passage up to a window, through which the moonlight was shining. Here I released my hold of his throat, but immediately covered him with my revolver.

"Down on your knees, or you are a dead man!" I cried. "Confess everything, or I shoot you through the heart."

His courage had evidently forsaken him; he began to whimper and cry bitterly.

"Spare my life," he screamed. "I will tell everything, only spare my life."

"Be quick about it," I said; "I am in no humour to be merciful. Out with the truth."

I was listening anxiously for the wife's step, but except for the low hum of machinery and the splashing of the water I heard nothing.

"Speak," I said, giving the old man a shake. His lips trembled, his words came out falteringly.

"It was Wentworth's doing," he panted.

"Wentworth? Not the murdered man?" I cried.

"No, no, his cousin. The ruffian who has been the curse of my life. Owing to that last death he inherits the property. He is the real owner of the mill, and he invented the revolving floor. There were deaths—oh yes, oh yes. It was so easy, and I wanted the money. The police never suspected, nor did the doctors. Wentworth was bitter hard on me, and I got into his power." Here he choked and sobbed. "I am a miserable old man, sir," he gasped.

"So you killed your victims for the sake of money?" I said, grasping him by the shoulder.

"Yes," he said, "yes. The bailiff had twenty pounds all in gold; no one ever knew. I took it and was able to satisfy Wentworth for a bit."

"And what about Archibald Wentworth?"

"That was *his* doing, and I was to be paid."

"And now finally you wanted to get rid of me?"

"Yes; for you suspected."

As I spoke I perceived by the ghastly light of the moon another door near. I opened it and saw that it was the entrance to a small dark lumber room. I pushed the old man in, turned the key in the lock, andran downstairs. The wife was still unaccountably absent. I opened the front door, and trembling, exhausted, drenched in perspiration, found myself in the open air. Every nerve was shaken. At that terrible moment I was not in the least master of myself. My one desire was to fly from the hideous place. I had just reached the little gate when a hand, light as a feather, touched my arm. I looked up; the girl Liz stood before me.

"You are saved," she said; "thank God! I tried all I could to stop the wheel. See, I am drenched to the skin; I could not manage it. But at least I locked Grannie up. She's in the kitchen, sound asleep. She drank a lot of gin."

"Where were you all day yesterday?" I asked.

"Locked up in a room in the further tower, but I managed to squeeze through the window, although it half killed me. I knew if you stayed that they would try it on to-night. Thank God you are saved."

"Well, don't keep me now," I said; "I have been saved as by a miracle. You are a good girl; I am much obliged to you. You must tell me another time how you manage to live through all these horrors."

"Ain't I all but mad?" was her pathetic reply. "Oh, my God, what I suffer!" She pressed her hand to her face; the look in her eyes was terrible. But I could not wait now to talk to her further. I hastily left the place.

How I reached Harkhurst I can never tell, but early in the morning I found myself there. I went straight to Dr. Stanmore's house, and having got him up, I communicated my story. He and I together immediately visited the superintendent of police. Having told my exciting tale, we took a trap and all three returned to the Castle Inn. We were back there before eight o'clock on the following morning. But as the police officer expected, the place was empty. Bindloss had been rescued from the dark closet, and he and his wife and the girl Liz had all flown. The doctor, the police officer, and I, all went up to the circular room. We then descended to the basement, and after a careful examination we discovered a low door, through which we crept; we then found ourselves in a dark vault, which was full of machinery. By the light of a lantern we examined it. Here we saw an explanation of the whole trick. The shaft of the mill-wheel which was let through the wall of the tower was *continuous as the axle of a vertical cogged wheel*, and by a multiplication action turned a large horizontal wheel into which a vertical shaft descended. This shaft was let into the centre of four crossbeams, sup-porting the floor of the room in which I had slept. All round the circular edge of the floor was a steel rim which turned in a circular socket. It needed but a touch to set this hideous apparatus in motion.

The police immediately started in pursuit of Bindloss, and I returned to London. That evening Edgcombe and I visited Dr. Miles Gordon. Hard-headed old physician that he was, he was literally aghast when I told him my story. He explained to me that a man placed in the position in which I was when the floor began to move would by means of centrifugal force suffer from enormous congestion of the brain. In fact, the revolving floor would induce an artificial condition of apo-plexy. If the victim were drugged or even only sleeping heav-ily, and the floor began to move slowly, insensibility would almost immediately be induced, which would soon pass into coma and death, and a post-mortem examination some hours afterwards would show no cause for death, as the brain would appear perfectly healthy, the blood having again left it.

From the presence of Dr. Miles Gordon, Edgcombe and I went to Scotland Yard, and the whole affair was put into the hands of the London detective force. With the clue which I had almost sacrificed my life to furnish, they quickly did the rest. Wentworth was arrested, and under pressure was induced to make a full confession, but old Bindloss had already told me the gist of the story. Wentworth's father had owned the mill, had got into trouble with the law, and changed his name. In fact, he had spent five years in penal servitude. He then went to Australia and made money. He died when his son was a young man. This youth inherited all the father's vices. He came home, visited the mill, and, being of a mechanical turn of mind, invented the revolving floor. He changed the mill into an inn, put Bindloss, one of his "pals," into possession with the full intention of murdering unwary travellers from time to time for their money.

The police, however, wanted him for a forged bill, and he thought it best to fly. Bindloss was left in full possession. Worried by Wentworth, who had him in his power for a grave crime committed years ago, he himself on two occasions murdered a victim in the circular room. Meanwhile several unexpected deaths had taken place in the older branch of the Wentworth family, and Archibald Wentworth alone stood between his cousin and the great estates. Wentworth came home, and with the aid of Bindloss got Archibald into his power. The young artist slept in the fatal room, and his death was the result. At this moment Wentworth and Bindloss are committed for trial at the Old Bailey, and there is no doubt what the result will be.

The ghost mystery in connection with the Castle Inn has, of course, been explained away for ever.

THE WARDER OF THE DOOR

"If you don't believe it, you can read it for yourself," said Allen Clinton, climbing up the steps and searching among the volumes on the top shelf.

I lay back in my chair. The beams from the sinking sun shone through the stained glass of the windows of the old library, and dyed the rows of black leather volumes with bands of red and yellow.

"Here, Bell!"

I took a musty volume from Allen Clinton, which he had unearthed from its resting-place.

"It is about the middle of the book," he continued eagerly. "You will see it in big, black, old English letters."

I turned over the pages containing the family tree and other archives of the Clintons till I came to the one I was seeking. It contained the curse which had rested on the family since 1400. Slowly and with difficulty I deciphered the words of this terrible denunciation.

"And in this cell its coffin lieth, the coffin which hath not human shape, for which reason no holy ground receiveth it. Here shall it rest to curse the family of ye Clyntons from generation to generation. And for this reason, as soon as the soul shall pass from the body of each first-born, which is the heir, it shall become the warder of the door by day and by night. Day and night shall his spirit stand by the door, to keep the door closed till the son shall release the spirit of the father from the watch and take his place, till his son in turn shall die. And whoso entereth into the cell shall be the prisoner of the soul that guardeth the door till it shall let him go."

"What a ghastly idea!" I said, glancing up at the young man who was watching me as I read. "But you say this cell has never been found. I should say its existence was a myth, and, of course, the curse on the soul of the first-born to keep the door shut as warder is absurd. Matter does not obey witch-craft."

"The odd part of it is," replied Allen, "that every other detail of the Abbey referred to in this record has been identified; but this cell with its horrible contents has never been found."

It certainly was a curious legend, and I allow it made some impression on me. I fancied, too, that somewhere I had heard something similar, but my memory failed to trace it.

I had come down to Clinton Abbey three days before for some pheasant shooting.

It was now Sunday afternoon. The family, with the exception of old Sir Henry, Allen, and myself, were at church. Sir Henry, now nearly eighty years of age and a chronic invalid, had retired to his room for his afternoon sleep. The younger Clinton and I had gone out for a stroll round the grounds, and since we returned our conversation had run upon the family history till it arrived at the legend of the family curse. Presently, the door of the library was slowly opened, and Sir Henry, in his black velvet coat, which formed such a striking contrast to his snowy white beard and hair, entered the room. I rose from my chair, and, giving him my arm, assisted him to his favourite couch. He sank down into its luxurious depths with a sigh, but as he did so his eyes caught the old volume which I had laid on the table beside it. He started forward, took the book in his hand, and looked across at his son.

"Did you take this book down?" he said sharply.

"Yes, father; I got it out to show it to Bell. He is interested in the history of the Abbey, and——"

"Then return it to its place at once," interrupted the old man, his black eyes blazing with sudden passion. "You know how I dislike having my books disarranged, and this one above all. Stay, give it to me."

He struggled up from the couch, and, taking the volume, locked it up in one of the drawers of his writing-table, and then sat back again on the sofa. His hands were trembling, as if some sudden fear had taken possession of him.

"Did you say that Phyllis Curzon is coming to-morrow?" asked the old man presently of his son in an irritable voice.

"Yes, father, of course; don't you remember? Mrs. Curzon and Phyllis are coming to stay for a fortnight; and, by the way," he added, starting to his feet as he spoke, "that reminds me I must go and tell Grace——"

The rest of the sentence was lost in the closing of the door. As soon as we were alone, Sir Henry looked across at me for a few moments without speaking. Then he said,—

"I am sorry I was so short just now. I am not myself. I do not know what is the matter with me. I feel all to pieces. I cannot sleep. I do not think my time is very long now, and I am worried about Allen. The fact is, I would give anything to stop this engagement. I wish he would not marry."

"I am sorry to hear you say that, sir," I answered. "I should have thought you would have been anxious to see your son happily married."

"Most men would," was the reply; "but I have my reasons for wishing things otherwise."

"What do you mean?" I could not help asking.

"I cannot explain myself; I wish I could. It would be best for Allen to let the old family die out. There, perhaps I am foolish about it, and of course I cannot really stop the marriage, but I am worried and troubled about many things."

"I wish I could help you, sir," I said impulsively. "If there is anything I can possibly do, you know you have only to ask me."

"Thank you, Bell, I know you would; but I cannot tell you. Some day I may. But there, I am afraid—horribly afraid."

The trembling again seized him, and he put his hands over his eyes as if to shut out some terrible sight.

"Don't repeat a word of what I have told you to Allen or any one else," he said suddenly. "It is possible that some day I may ask you to help me; and remember, Bell, I trust you."

He held out his hand, which I took. In another moment the butler entered with the lamps, and I took advantage of the interruption to make my way to the drawing-room.

The next day the Curzons arrived, and a hasty glance showed me that Phyllis was a charming girl. She was tall, slightly built, with a figure both upright and graceful, and a handsome, somewhat proud face. When in perfect repose her expression was somewhat haughty; but the moment she spoke her face became vivacious, kindly, charming to an extraordinary degree; she had a gay laugh, a sweet smile, a sympathetic manner. I was certain she had the kindest of hearts, and was sure that Allen had made an admirable choice.

A few days went by, and at last the evening before the day when I was to return to London arrived. Phyllis's mother had gone to bed a short time before, as she had complained of headache, and Allen suddenly proposed, as the night was a perfect one, that we should go out and enjoy a moonlight stroll.

Phyllis laughed with glee at the suggestion, and ran at once into the hall to take a wrap from one of the pegs.

"Allen," she said to her lover, who was following her, "you and I will go first."

"No, young lady, on this occasion you and I will have that privilege," said Sir Henry. He had also come into the hall, and, to our astonishment, announced his intention of accompanying us in our walk.

Phyllis bestowed upon him a startled glance, then she laid her hand lightly on his arm, nodded back at Allen with a smile, and walked on in front somewhat rapidly. Allen and I followed in the rear.

"Now, what does my father mean by this?" said Allen to me. "He never goes out at night; but he has not been well lately. I sometimes think he grows queerer every day."

"He is very far from well, I am certain," I answered.

We stayed out for about half an hour and returned home by a path which led into the house through a side entrance. Phyllis was waiting for us in the hall.

"Where is my father?" asked Allen, going up to her.

"He is tired and has gone to bed," she answered. "Good-night, Allen."

"Won't you come into the drawing-room?" he asked in some astonishment.

"No, I am tired."

She nodded to him without touching his hand; her eyes, I could not help noticing, had a queer expression. She ran upstairs.

I saw that Allen was startled by her manner; but as he did not say anything, neither did I.

The next day at breakfast I was told that the Curzons had already left the Abbey. Allen was full of astonishment and, I could see, a good deal annoyed. He and I breakfasted alone in the old library. His father was too ill to come downstairs.

An hour later I was on my way back to London. Many things there engaged my immediate attention, and Allen, his engagement, Sir Henry, and the old family curse, sank more or less into the background of my mind.

Three months afterwards, on the 7th of January, I saw to my sorrow in the *Times* the announcement of Sir Henry Clinton's death.

From time to time in the interim I had heard from the son, saying that his father was failing fast. He further mentioned that his own wedding was fixed for the twenty-first of the present month. Now, of course, it must be postponed. I felt truly sorry for Allen, and wrote immediately a long letter of condolence.

On the following day I received a wire from him, imploring me to go down to the Abbey as soon as possible, saying that he was in great difficulty.

I packed a few things hastily, and arrived at Clinton Abbey at six in the evening. The house was silent and subdued—the funeral was to take place the next day. Clinton came into the hall and gripped me warmly by the hand. I noticed at once how worn and worried he looked.

"This is good of you, Bell," he said. "I cannot tell you how grateful I am to you for coming. You are the one man who can help me, for I know you have had much experience in matters of this sort. Come into the library and I will tell you everything. We shall dine alone this evening, as my mother and the girls are keeping to their own apartments for to-night."

As soon as we were seated, he plunged at once into his story.

"I must give you a sort of prelude to what has just occurred," he began. "You remember, when you were last here, how abruptly Phyllis and her mother left the Abbey?"

I nodded. I remembered well.

"On the morning after you had left us I had a long letter from Phyllis," continued Allen. "In it she told me of an extraordinary request my father had made to her during that moonlight walk—nothing more nor less than an earnest wish that she would herself terminate our engagement. She spoke quite frankly, as she always does, assuring me of her unalterable love and devotion, but saying that under the circumstances it was absolutely necessary to have an explanation. Frantic with almost ungovernable rage, I sought my father in his study. I laid Phyllis's letter before him and asked him what it meant. He looked at me with the most unutterable expression of weariness and pathos.

"'Yes, my boy, I did it,' he said. 'Phyllis is quite right. I did ask of her, as earnestly as a very old man could plead, that she would bring the engagement to an end.'

"'But why?' I asked. 'Why?'

"'That I am unable to tell you,' he replied.

"I lost my temper and said some words to him which I now regret. He made no sort of reply. When I had done speaking he said slowly,—

"'I make all allowance for your emotion, Allen; your feelings are no more than natural.'

"'You have done me a very sore injury,' I retorted. 'What can Phyllis think of this? She will never be the same again. I am going to see her to-day.'

"He did not utter another word, and I left him. I was absent from home for about a week. It took me nearly that time to induce Phyllis to overlook my father's extraordinary request, and to let matters go on exactly as they had done before.

"After fixing our engagement, if possible, more firmly than ever, and also arranging the date of our wedding, I returned home. When I did so I told my father what I had done.

"'As you will,' he replied, and then he sank into great gloom. From that moment, although I watched him day and night, and did everything that love and tenderness could suggest, he never seemed to rally. He scarcely spoke, and remained, whenever we were together, bowed in deep and painful reverie. A week ago he took to his bed."

Here Allen paused.

"I now come to events up to date," he said. "Of course, as you may suppose, I was with my father to the last. A few hours before he passed away he called me to his bedside, and to my astonishment began once more talking about my engagement. He implored me with the utmost earnestness even now at the eleventh hour to break it off. It was not too late, he said, and added further that nothing would give him ease in dying but the knowledge that I would promise him to remain single. Of course I tried to humour him. He took my hand, looked me in the eyes with an expression which I shall never forget, and said,—

"'Allen, make me a solemn promise that you will never marry.'

"This I naturally had to refuse, and then he told me that, expecting my obstinacy, he had written me a letter which I should find in his safe, but I was not to open it till after his death. I found it this morning. Bell, it is the most extraordinary communication, and either it is entirely a figment of his imagination, for his brain powers were failing very much at the last, or else it is the most awful thing I ever heard of. Here is the letter; read it for yourself."

I took the paper from his hand and read the following matter in shaky, almost illegible writing:—

"My dear Boy,—

When you read this I shall have passed away. For the last six months my life has been a living death. The horror began in the following way. You know what a deep interest I have always taken in the family history of our house. I have spent the latter years of my life in verifying each detail, and my intention was, had health been given me, to publish a great deal of it in a suitable volume.

"On the special night to which I am about to allude, I sat up late in my study reading the book which I saw you show to Bell a short time ago. In particular, I was much attracted by the terrible curse which the old abbot in the fourteenth century had bestowed upon the family. I read the awful words again and again. I knew that all the other details in the volume had been verified, but that the vault with the coffin had never yet been found. Presently I grew drowsy, and I suppose I must have fallen asleep. In my sleep I had a dream; I thought that some one came into the room, touched me on the shoulder, and said 'Come.' I looked up; a tall figure beckoned to me. The voice and the figure belonged to my late father. In my dream I rose immediately, although I did not know why I went nor where I was going. The figure went on in front, it entered the hall. I took one of the candles from the table and the key of the chapel, unbolted the door and went out. Still the voice kept saying 'Come, come,' and the figure of my father walked in front of me. I went across the quadrangle, unlocked the chapel door, and entered.

"A death-like silence was around me. I crossed the nave to the north aisle; the figure still went in front of me; it entered the great pew which is said to be haunted, and walked straight up to the effigy of the old abbot who had pronounced the curse. This, as you know, is built into the opposite wall. Bending forward, the figure pressed the eyes of the old monk, and immediately a stone started out of its place, revealing a staircase behind. I was about to hurry forward, when I must have knocked against something. I felt a sensation of pain, and suddenly awoke. What was my amazement to find that I had acted on my dream, had crossed the quadrangle, and was in the chapel; in fact, was standing in the old pew! Of course there was no figure of any sort visible, but the moonlight shed a cold radiance over all the place. I felt very much startled and impressed, but was just about to return to the house in some wonder at the curious vision which I had experienced, when, raising my startled eyes, I saw that part of it at least was real. The old monk seemed to grin at me from his marble effigy, and beside him was a *blank open space*. I hurried to it and saw a narrow flight of stairs. I cannot explain what my emotions were, but my keenest feeling at that moment was a strong and horrible curiosity. Holding the candle in my hand, I went down the steps. They terminated at the beginning of a long passage. This I quickly traversed, and at last found myself beside an iron door. It was not locked, but hasped, and was very hard to open; in fact, it required nearly all my strength; at last I pulled it open towards me, and there in a small cell lay the coffin, as the words of the curse said. I gazed at it in horror. I did not dare to enter. It was a wedged-shaped coffin studded with great nails. But as I looked my blood froze within me, for slowly, very slowly, as if pushed by some unseen hand, the great heavy door began to close, quicker and quicker, until with a crash that echoed and re-echoed through the empty vault, it shut.

"Terror-stricken, I rushed from the vault and reached my room once more.

"Now I know that this great curse is true; that my father's spirit is there to guard the door and close it, for I saw it with my own eyes, and while you read this know that I am there. I charge you, therefore, not to marry—bring no child into the world to perpetuate this terrible curse. Let the family die out if you have the courage. It is much, I know, to ask; but whether you do or not, come to me there, and if by sign or word I can communicate with you I will do so, but hold the secret safe. Meet me there before my body is laid to rest, when body and soul are still not far from each other. Farewell.

—Your loving father,
"HENRY CLINTON."

I read this strange letter over carefully twice, and laid it down. For a moment I hardly knew what to say. It was certainly the most uncanny thing I had ever come across.

"What do you think of it?" asked Allen at last.

"Well, of course there are only two possible solutions," I answered. "One is that your father not only dreamt the beginning of this story—which, remember, he allows himself—but the whole of it."

"And the other?" asked Allen, seeing that I paused.

"The other," I continued, "I hardly know what to say yet. Of course we will investigate the whole thing, that is our only chance of arriving at a solution. It is absurd to let matters rest as they are. We had better try to-night."

Clinton winced and hesitated.

"Something must be done, of course," he answered; "but the worst of it is Phyllis and her mother are coming here early to-morrow in time for the funeral, and I cannot meet her—no, I cannot, poor girl!—while I feel as I do."

"We will go to the vault to-night," I said.

Clinton rose from his chair and looked at me.

"I don't like this thing at all, Bell," he continued. "I am not by nature in any sense of the word a superstitious man, but I tell you frankly nothing would induce me to go alone into that chapel to-night; if you come with me, that, of course, alters matters. I know the pew my father refers to well; it is beneath the window of St. Sebastian."

Soon afterwards I went to my room and dressed; and Allen and I dined *tête-à-tête* in the great dining-room. The old butler waited on us with funereal solemnity, and I did all I could to lure Clinton's thoughts into a more cheerful and healthier channel.

I cannot say that I was very successful. I further noticed that he scarcely ate anything, and seemed altogether to be in a state of nervous tension painful to witness.

After dinner we went into the smoking-room, and at eleven o'clock I proposed that we should make a start.

Clinton braced himself together and we went out. He got the chapel keys, and then going to the stables we borrowed a lantern, and a moment afterwards found ourselves in the sacred edifice. The moon was at her full, and by the pale light which was diffused through the south windows the architecture of the interior could be faintly seen. The Gothic arches that flanked the centre aisle with their quaint pillars, each with a carved figure of one of the saints, were quite visible, and further in the darkness of the chancel the dim outlines of the choir and altar-table with its white marble reredos could be just discerned.

We closed the door softly and, Clinton leading the way with the lantern, we walked up the centre aisle paved with the brasses of his dead ancestors. We trod gently on tiptoe as one instinctively does at night. Turning beneath the little pulpit we reached the north transept, and here Clinton stopped and turned round. He was very white, but his voice was quiet.

"This is the pew," he whispered. "It has always been called the haunted pew of Sir Hugh Clinton."

I took the lantern from him and we entered. I crossed the pew immediately and went up to the effigy of the old abbot.

"Let us examine him closely," I said. I held up the lantern, getting it to shine on each part of the face, the vestments, and the figure. The eyes, although vacant, as in all statuary, seemed to me at that moment to be uncanny and peculiar. Giving Allen the lantern to hold, I placed a finger firmly on each. The next moment I could not refrain from an exclamation; a stone at the side immediately rolled back, revealing the steps which were spoken of by the old man in his narrative.

"It is true! It is true!" cried Clinton excitedly.

"It certainly looks like it," I remarked: "but never mind, we have the chance now of investigating this matter thoroughly."

"Are you going down?" asked Clinton.

"Certainly I am," I replied. "Let us go together."

Immediately afterwards we crept through the opening and began to descend. There was only just room to do so in single file, and I went first with the lantern. In another moment we were in the long passage, and soon we were confronted by a door in an arched stone framework. Up till now Clinton had shown little sign of alarm, but here, at the trysting-place to which his father's soul had summoned him, he seemed suddenly to lose his nerve. He leant against the wall and for a moment I thought he would have fallen. I held up the lantern and examined the door and walls carefully. Then approaching I lifted the iron latch ofthe heavy door. It was very hard to move, but at last by seizing the edge I dragged it open to its full against the wall of the passage. Having done so I peered inside, holding the lantern above my head. As I did so I heard Clinton cry out,—

"Look, look," he said, and turning I saw that the great door had swung back against me, almost shutting me within the cell.

Telling Clinton to hold it back by force, I stepped inside and saw at my feet the ghastly coffin. The legend then so far was true. I bent down and examined the queer, misshapen thing with great care. Its shape was that of an enormous wedge, and it was apparently made of some dark old wood, and was bound with iron at the corners. Having looked at it all round, I went out and, flinging back the door which Clinton had been holding open, stood aside to watch. Slowly, very slowly, as we both stood in the passage—slowly, as if pushed by some invisible hand, the door commenced to swing round, and, increasing in velocity, shut with a noisy clang.

Seizing it once again, I dragged it open and, while Clinton held it in that position, made a careful examination. Up to the present I saw nothing to be much alarmed about. There were fifty ways in which a door might shut of its own accord. There might be a hidden spring or tilted hinges; draught, of course, was out of the question. I looked at the hinges, they were of iron and set in the solid masonry. Nor could I discover any spring or hidden contrivance, as when the door was wide open there was an interval of several inches between it and the wall. We tried it again and again with the same result, and at last, as it was closing, I seized it to prevent it.

I now experienced a very odd sensation; I certainly felt as if I were resisting an unseen person who was pressing hard against the door at the other side. Directly it was released it continued its course. I allow I was quite unable to understand the mystery. Suddenly an idea struck me.

"What does the legend say?" I asked, turning to Clinton. "'That the soul is to guard the door, to close it upon the coffin?'"

"Those are the words," answered Allen, speaking with some difficulty.

"Now if that is true," I continued, "and we take the coffin out, the spirit won't shut the door; if it does shut it, it disproves the whole thing at once, and shows it to be merely a clever mechanical contrivance. Come, Clinton, help me to get the coffin out."

"I dare not, Bell," he whispered hoarsely. "I daren't go inside."

"Nonsense, man," I said, feeling now a little annoyed at the whole thing. "Here, put the lantern down and hold the door back." I stepped in and, getting behind the coffin, put out all my strength and shoved it into the passage.

"Now, then," I cried, "I'll bet you fifty pounds to five the door will shut just the same." I dragged the coffin clear of the door and told him to let go. Clinton had scarcely done so before, stepping back, he clutched my arm.

"Look," he whispered; "do you see that it will not shut now? My father is waiting for the coffin to be put back. This is awful!"

I gazed at the door in horror; it was perfectly true, it remained wide open, and quite still. I sprang forward, seized it, and now endeavoured to close it. It was as if some one was trying to hold it open; it required considerable force to stir it, and it was only with difficulty I could move it at all. At last I managed to shut it, but the moment I let go it swung back open of its own accord and struck against the wall, where it remained just as before. In the dead silence that followed I could hear Clinton breathing quickly behind me, and I knew he was holding himself for all he was worth.

At that moment there suddenly came over me a sensation which I had once experienced before, and which I was twice destined to experience again. It is impossible to describe it, but it seized me, laying siege to my brain till I felt like a child in its power. It was as if I were slowly drowning in the great ocean of silence that enveloped us. Time itself seemed to have disappeared. At my feet lay the misshapen thing, and the lantern behind it cast a fantastic shadow of its distorted outline on the cell wall before me.

"Speak; say something," I cried to Clinton. The sharp sound of my voice broke the spell. I felt myself again, and smiled at the trick my nerves had played on me. I bent down and once more laid my hands on the coffin, but before I had time to push it back into its place Clinton had gone up the passage like a man who is flying to escape a hurled javelin.

Exerting all my force to prevent the door from swinging back by keeping my leg against it, I had just got the coffin into the cell and was going out, when I heard a shrill cry, and Clinton came tearing back down the passage.

"I can't get out! The stone has sunk into its place! We are locked in!" he screamed, and, wild with fear, he plunged headlong into the cell, upsetting me in his career before I could check him. I sprang back to the door as it was closing. I was too late. Before I could reach it, it had shut with a loud clang in obedience to the infernal witchcraft.

"You have done it now," I cried angrily. "Do you see? Why, man, we are buried alive in this ghastly hole!"

The lantern I had placed just inside the door, and by its dim light, as I looked at him, I saw the terror of a madman creep into Clinton's eyes.

"Buried alive!" he shouted, with a peal of hysterical laughter. "Yes, and, Bell, it's your doing; you are a devil in human shape!" With a wild paroxysm of fury he flung himself upon me. There was the ferocity of a wild beast in his spring. He upset the lantern and left us in total darkness.

The struggle was short. We might be buried alive, but I was not going to die by his hand, and seizing him by the throat I pinned him against the wall.

"Keep quiet," I shouted. "It is your thundering stupidity that has caused all this. Stay where you are until I strike a match."

I luckily had some vestas in the little silver box which I always carry on my watch-chain, and striking one I relit the lantern. Clinton's paroxysm was over, and sinking to the floor he lay there shivering and cowering.

It was a terrible situation, and I knew that our only hope was for me to keep my presence of mind. With a great effort I forced myself to think calmly over what could be done. To shout for help would have been but a useless waste of breath.

Suddenly an idea struck me. "Have you got your father's letter?" I cried eagerly.

"I have," he answered; "it is in my pocket."

My last ray of hope vanished. Our only chance was that if he had left it at the house some one might discover the letter and come to our rescue by its instructions. It had been a faint hope, and it disappeared almost as quickly as it had come to me. Without it no one would ever find the way to the vault that had remained a secret for ages. I was determined, however, not to die without a struggle for freedom. Taking the lantern, I examined every nook and cranny of the cell for some other exit. It was a fruitless search. No sign of any way out could I find, and we had absolutely no means to unfasten the door from the inner side. Taking a few short steps, I flung myself again and again at the heavy door. It never budged an inch, and, bruised and sweating at every pore, I sat down on the coffin and tried to collect all my faculties.

Clinton was silent, and seemed utterly stunned. He sat still, gazing with a vacant stare at the door.

The time dragged heavily, and there was nothing to do but to wait for a horrible death from starvation. It was more than likely, too, that Clinton would go mad; already his nerves were strained to the utmost. Altogether I had never found myself in a worse plight.

It seemed like an eternity that we sat there, neither of us speaking a word. Over and over again I repeated to myself the words of the terrible curse: "And whoso entereth into the cell shall be the prisoner of the soul that guardeth the door till it shall let him go." When would the shapeless form that was inside the coffin let us go? Doubtless when our bones were dry.

I looked at my watch. It was half-past eleven o'clock. Surely we had been more than ten minutes in this awful place! We had left the house at eleven, and I knew that must have been many hours ago. I glanced at the second hand. *The watch had stopped.*

"What is the time, Clinton?" I asked. "My watch has stopped."

"What does it matter?" he murmured. "What is time to us now? The sooner we die the better."

He pulled out his watch as he spoke, and held it to the lantern.

"Twenty-five minutes past eleven," he murmured dreamily.

"Good heavens!" I cried, starting up. "Has your watch stopped, too?"

Then, like the leap of a lightning flash, an idea struck me.

"I have got it; I have got it! My God! I believe I have got it!" I cried, seizing him by the arm.

"Got what?" he replied, staring wildly at me.

"Why, the secret—the curse—the door. Don't you see?"

I pulled out the large knife I always carry by a chain and swivel in my trouser pocket, and telling Clinton to hold the lantern, opened the little blade-saw and attacked the coffin with it.

"I believe the secret of our deliverance lies in this," I panted, working away furiously.

In ten minutes I had sawn half through the wooden edge, then, handing my tool to Clinton, I told him to continue the work while I rested. After a few minutes I took the knife again, and at last, after nearly half an hour had gone by, succeeded in making a small hole in the lid. Inserting my two fingers, I felt some rough, uneven masses. I was now fearfully excited. Tearing at the opening like a madman, I enlarged it and extracted what looked like a large piece of coal. I knew in an instant what it was. It was magnetic iron-ore. Holding it down to my knife, the blade flew to it.

"Here is the mystery of the soul," I cried; "now we can use it to open the door."

I had known a great conjurer once, who had deceived and puzzled his audience with a box trick on similar lines: the man opening the box from the inside by drawing down the lock with a magnet. Would this do the same? I felt that our lives hung on the next moment. Taking the mass, I pressed it against the door just opposite the hasp, and slid it up against the wood. My heart leapt as I heard the hasp fly up outside, and with a push the door opened.

"We are saved," I shouted. "We are saved by a miracle!"

"Bell, you are a genius," gasped poor Clinton; "but now, how about the stone at the end of the passage?"

"We will soon see about that," I cried, taking the lantern. "Half the danger is over, at any rate; and the worst half, too."

We rushed along the passage and up the stair until we reached the top.

"Why, Clinton," I cried, holding up the lantern, "the place was not shut at all."

Nor was it. In his terror he had imagined it.

"I could not see in the dark, and I was nearly dead with fright," he said. "Oh, Bell, let us get out of this as quickly as we can!"

We crushed through the aperture and once more stood in the chapel. I then pushed the stone back into its place.

Dawn was just breaking when we escaped from the chapel. We hastened across to the house. In the hall the clock pointed to five.

"Well, we have had an awful time," I said, as we stood in the hall together; "but at least, Clinton, the end was worth the ghastly terror. I have knocked the bottom out of your family legend for ever."

"I don't even now quite understand," he said.

"Don't you?—but it is so easy. That coffin never contained a body at all, but was filled, as you perceive, with fragments of magnetic iron-ore. For what diabolical purposes the cell was intended, it is, of course, impossible to say; but that it must have been meant as a human trap there is little doubt. The inventor certainly exercised no small ingenuity when he devised his diabolical plot, for it was obvious that the door, which was made of iron, would swing towards the coffin wherever it happened to be placed. Thus the door would shut if the coffin were *inside the cell*, and would remain open if the coffin were *brought out*. A cleverer method for simulating a spiritual agency it would be hard to find. Of course, the monk must have known well that magnetic iron-ore never loses its quality and would ensure the deception remaining potent for ages."

"But how did you discover by means of our watches?" asked Clinton.

"Any one who understands magnetism can reply to that," I said. "It is a well-known fact that a strong magnet plays havoc with watches. The fact of both our watches going wrong first gave me a clue to the mystery."

Later in the day the whole of this strange affair was explained to Miss Curzon, and not long afterwards the passage and entrance to the chapel were bricked up.

It is needless to add that six months later the pair were married, and, I believe, are as happy as they deserve.

THE MYSTERY OF THE FELWYN TUNNEL

I was making experiments of some interest at South Kensington, and hoped that I had perfected a small but not unimportant discovery, when, on returning home one evening in late October in the year 1893, I found a visiting card on my table. On it were inscribed the words, "Mr. Geoffrey Bainbridge." This name was quite unknown to me, so I rang the bell and inquired of my servant who the visitor had been. He described him as a gentleman who wished to see me on most urgent business, and said further that Mr. Bainbridge intended to call again later in the evening. It was with both curiosity and vexation that I awaited the return of the stranger. Urgent business with me generally meant a hurried rush to one part of the country or the other. I did not want to leave London just then; and when at half-past nine Mr. Geoffrey Bainbridge was ushered into my room, I received him with a certain coldness which he could not fail to perceive. He was a tall, well-dressed, elderly man. He immediately plunged into the object of his visit.

"I hope you do not consider my unexpected presence an intrusion, Mr. Bell," he said. "But I have heard of you from our mutual friends, the Greys of Uplands. You may remember once doing that family a great service."

"I remember perfectly well," I answered more cordially. "Pray tell me what you want; I shall listen with attention."

"I believe you are the one man in London who can help me," he continued. "I refer to a matter especially relating to your own particular study. I need hardly say that whatever you do will not be unrewarded."

"That is neither here nor there," I said; "but before you go any further, allow me to ask one question. Do you want me to leave London at present?"

He raised his eyebrows in dismay.

"I certainly do," he answered.

"Very well; pray proceed with your story."

He looked at me with anxiety.

"In the first place," he began, "I must tell you that I am chairman of the Lytton Vale Railway Company in Wales, and that it is on an important matter connected with our line that I have come to consult you. When I explain to you the nature of the mystery, you will not wonder, I think, at my soliciting your aid."

"I will give you my closest attention," I answered; and then I added, impelled to say the latter words by a certain expression on his face, "if I can see my way to assisting you I shall be ready to do so."

"Pray accept my cordial thanks," he replied. "I have come up from my place at Felwyn to-day on purpose to consult you. It is in that neighbourhood that the affair has occurred. As it is essential that you should be in possession of the facts of the whole matter, I will go over things just as they happened."

I bent forward and listened attentively.

"This day fortnight," continued Mr. Bainbridge, "our quiet little village was horrified by the news that the signalman on duty at the mouth of the Felwyn Tunnel had been found dead under the most mysterious circumstances. The tunnel is at the end of a long cutting between Llanlys and Felwyn stations. It is about a mile long, and the signal-box is on the Felwyn side. The place is extremely lonely, being six miles from the village across the mountains. The name of the poor fellow who met his death in this mysterious fashion was David Pritchard. I have known him from a boy, and he was quite one of the steadiest and most trustworthy men on the line. On Tuesday evening he went on duty at six o'clock; on Wednesday morning the day-man who had come to relieve him was surprised not to find him in the box. It was just getting daylight, and the 6.30 local was coming down, so he pulled the signals and let her through. Then he went out, and, looking up the line towards the tunnel, saw Pritchard lying beside the line close to the mouth of the tunnel. Roberts, the day-man, ran up to him and found, to his horror, that he was quite dead. At first Roberts naturally supposed that he had been cut down by a train, as there was a wound at the back of the head; but he was not lying on the metals. Roberts ran back to the box and telegraphed through to Felwyn Station. The message was sent on to the village, and at half-past seven o'clock the police inspector came up to my house with the news. He and I, with the local doctor, went off at once to the tunnel. We found the dead man lying beside the metals a few yards away from the mouth of the tunnel, and the doctor immediately gave him a careful examination. There was a depressed fracture at the back of the skull, which must have caused his death; but how he came by it was not so clear. On examining the whole place most carefully, we saw, further, that there were marks on the rocks at the steep side of the embankment as if some one had tried to scramble up them. Why the poor fellow had attempted such a climb, God only knows. In doing so he must have slipped and fallen back on to the line, thus causing the fracture of the skull. In no case could he have gone up more than eight or ten feet, as the banks of the cutting run sheer up, almost perpendicularly, beyond that point for more than a hundred and fifty feet. There are some sharp boulders beside the line, and it was possible that he might have fallen on one of these and so sustained the injury. The affair must have occurred some time between 11.45 p.m. and 6 a.m., as the engine-driver of the express at 11.45 p.m. states that the line was signalled clear, and he also caught sight of Pritchard in his box as he passed."

"This is deeply interesting," I said; "pray proceed."

Bainbridge looked at me earnestly; he then continued:—

"The whole thing is shrouded in mystery. Why should Pritchard have left his box and gone down to the tunnel? Why, having done so, should he have made a wild attempt to scale the side of the cutting, an impossible feat at any time? Had danger threatened, the ordinary course of things would have been to run up the line towards the signal-box. These points are quite unexplained. Another curious fact is that death appears to have taken place just before the day-man came on duty, as the light at the mouth of the tunnel had been put out, and it was one of the night signalman's duties to do this as soon as daylight appeared; it is possible, therefore, that Pritchard went down to the tunnel for that purpose. Against this theory, however, and an objection that seems to nullify it, is the evidence of Dr. Williams, who states that when he examined the body his opinion was that death had taken place some hours before. An inquest was held on the following day, but before it took place there was a new and most important development. I now come to what I consider the crucial point in the whole story.

"For a long time there had been a feud between Pritchard and another man of the name of Wynne, a platelayer on the line. The object of their quarrel was the blacksmith's daughter in the neighbouring village—a remarkably pretty girl and an arrant flirt. Both men were madly in love with her, and she played them off one against the other. The night but one before his death Pritchard and Wynne had met at the village inn, had quarrelled in the bar—Lucy, of course, being the subject of their difference. Wynne was heard to say (he was a man of powerful build and subject to fits of ungovernable rage) that he would have Pritchard's life. Pritchard swore a great oath that he would get Lucy on the following day to promise to marry him. This oath, it appears, he kept, and on his way to the signal-box on Tuesday evening met Wynne, and trium-phantly told him that Lucy had promised to be his wife. The men had a hand-to-hand fight on the spot, several people from the village being witnesses of it. They were separated with difficulty, each vowing vengeance on the other. Pritchard went off to his duty at the signal-box and Wynne returned to the village to drown his sorrows at the public-house.

"Very late that same night Wynne was seen by a villager going in the direction of the tunnel. The man stopped him and questioned him. He explained that he had left some of his tools on the line, and was on his way to fetch them. The villager noticed that he looked queer and excited, but not wishing to pick a quarrel thought it best not to question him further. It has been proved that Wynne never returned home that night, but came back at an early hour on the following morning, looking dazed and stupid. He was arrested on suspicion, and at the inquest the verdict was against him."

"Has he given any explanation of his own movements?" I asked.

"Yes; but nothing that can clear him. As a matter of fact, his tools were nowhere to be seen on the line, nor did he bring them home with him. His own story is that being considerably the worse for drink, he had fallen down in one of the fields and slept there till morning."

"Things look black against him," I said.

"They do; but listen, I have something more to add. Here comes a very queer feature in the affair. Lucy Ray, the girl who had caused the feud between Pritchard and Wynne, after hearing the news of Pritchard's death, completely lost her head, and ran frantically about the village declaring that Wynne was the man she really loved, and that she had only accepted Pritchard in a fit of rage with Wynne for not himself bringing matters to the point. The case looks very bad against Wynne, and yesterday the magistrate committed him for trial at the coming assizes. The unhappy Lucy Ray and the young man's parents are in a state bordering on distraction."

"What is your own opinion with regard to Wynne's guilt?" I asked.

"Before God, Mr. Bell, I believe the poor fellow is innocent, but the evidence against him is very strong. One of the favourite theories is that he went down to the tunnel and extinguished the light, knowing that this would bring Pritchard out of his box to see what was the matter, and that he then attacked him, striking the blow which fractured the skull."

"Has any weapon been found about, with which he could have given such a blow?"

"No; nor has anything of the kind been discovered on Wynne's person; that fact is decidedly in his favour."

"But what about the marks on the rocks?" I asked.

"It is possible that Wynne may have made them in order to divert suspicion by making people think that Pritchard must have fallen, and so killed himself. The holders of this theory base their belief on the absolute want of cause for Pritchard's trying to scale the rock. The whole thing is the most absolute enigma. Some of the country folk have declared that the tunnel is haunted (and there certainly has been such a rumour current among them for years). That Pritchard saw some apparition, and in wild terror sought to escape from it by climbing the rocks, is another theory, but only the most imaginative hold it."

"Well, it is a most extraordinary case," I replied.

"Yes, Mr. Bell, and I should like to get your opinion of it. Do you see your way to elucidate the mystery?"

"Not at present; but I shall be happy to investigate the matter to my utmost ability."

"But you do not wish to leave London at present?"

"That is so; but a matter of such importance cannot be set aside. It appears, from what you say, that Wynne's life hangs more or less on my being able to clear away the mystery?"

"That is indeed the case. There ought not to be a single stone left unturned to get at the truth, for the sake of Wynne. Well, Mr. Bell, what do you propose to do?"

"To see the place without delay," I answered.

"That is right; when can you come?"

"Whenever you please."

"Will you come down to Felwyn with me to-morrow? I shall leave Paddington by the 7.10, and if you will be my guest I shall be only too pleased to put you up."

"That arrangement will suit me admirably," I replied. "I will meet you by the train you mention, and the affair shall have my best attention."

"Thank you," he said, rising. He shook hands with me and took his leave.

The next day I met Bainbridge at Paddington Station, and we were soon flying westward in the luxurious private compartment that had been reserved for him. I could see by his abstracted manner and his long lapses of silence that the mysterious affair at Felwyn Tunnel was occupying all his thoughts.

It was two o'clock in the afternoon when the train slowed down at the little station of Felwyn. The station-master was at the door in an instant to receive us.

"I have some terribly bad news for you, sir," he said, turning to Bainbridge as we alighted; "and yet in one sense it is a relief, for it seems to clear Wynne."

"What do you mean?" cried Bainbridge. "Bad news? Speak out at once!"

"Well, sir, it is this: there has been another death at Felwyn signal-box. John Davidson, who was on duty last night, was found dead at an early hour this morning in the very same place where we found poor Pritchard."

"Good God!" cried Bainbridge, starting back, "what an awful thing! What, in the name of Heaven, does it mean, Mr. Bell? This is too fearful. Thank goodness you have come down with us."

"It is as black a business as I ever heard of, sir," echoed the station-master; "and what we are to do I don't know. Poor Davidson was found dead this morning, and there was neither mark nor sign of what killed him—that is the extraordinary part of it. There's a perfect panic abroad, and not a signal-man on the line will take duty to-night. I was quite in despair, and was afraid at one time that the line would have to be closed, but at last it occurred to me to wire to Lytton Vale, and they are sending down an inspector. I expect him by a special every moment. I believe this is he coming now," added the station-master, looking up the line.

There was the sound of a whistle down the valley, and in a few moments a single engine shot into the station, and an official in uniform stepped on to the platform.

"Good-evening, sir," he said, touching his cap to Bainbridge; "I have just been sent down to inquire into this affair at the Felwyn Tunnel, and though it seems more of a matter for a Scotland Yard detective than one of ourselves, there was nothing for it but to come. All the same, Mr. Bainbridge, I cannot say that I look forward to spending to-night alone at the place."

"You wish for the services of a detective, but you shall have some one better," said Bainbridge, turning towards me. "This gentleman, Mr. John Bell, is the man of all others for our business. I have just brought him down from London for the purpose."

An expression of relief flitted across the inspector's face.

"I am very glad to see you, sir," he said to me, "and I hope you will be able to spend the night with me in the signal-box. I must say I don't much relish the idea of tackling the thing single-handed; but with your help, sir, I think we ought to get to the bottom of it somehow. I am afraid there is not a man on the line who will take duty until we do. So it is most important that the thing should be cleared, and without delay."

I readily assented to the inspector's proposition, and Bainbridge and I arranged that we should call for him at four o'clock at the village inn and drive him to the tunnel.

We then stepped into the wagonette which was waiting for us, and drove to Bainbridge's house.

Mrs. Bainbridge came out to meet us, and was full of the tragedy. Two pretty girls also ran to greet their father, and to glance inquisitively at me. I could see that the entire family was in a state of much excitement.

"Lucy Ray has just left, father," said the elder of the girls. "We had much trouble to soothe her; she is in a frantic state."

"You have heard, Mr. Bell, all about this dreadful mystery?" said Mrs. Bainbridge as she led me towards the dining-room.

"Yes," I answered; "your husband has been good enough to give me every particular."

"And you have really come here to help us?"

"I hope I may be able to discover the cause," I answered.

"It certainly seems most extraordinary," continued Mrs. Bainbridge. "My dear," she continued, turning to her husband, "you can easily imagine the state we were all in this morning when the news of the second death was brought to us."

"For my part," said Ella Bainbridge, "I am sure that Felwyn Tunnel is haunted. The villagers have thought so for a long time, and this second death seems to prove it, does it not?" Here she looked anxiously at me.

"I can offer no opinion," I replied, "until I have sifted the matter thoroughly."

"Come, Ella, don't worry Mr. Bell," said her father; "if he is as hungry as I am, he must want his lunch."

We then seated ourselves at the table and commenced the meal. Bainbridge, although he professed to be hungry, was in such a state of excitement that he could scarcely eat. Immediately after lunch he left me to the care of his family and went into the village.

"It is just like him," said Mrs. Bainbridge; "he takes these sort of things to heart dreadfully. He is terribly upset about Lucy Ray, and also about the poor fellow Wynne. It is certainly a fearful tragedy from first to last."

"Well, at any rate," I said, "this fresh death will upset the evidence against Wynne."

"I hope so, and there is some satisfaction in the fact. Well, Mr. Bell, I see you have finished lunch; will you come into the drawing-room?"

I followed her into a pleasant room overlooking the valley of the Lytton.

By-and-by Bainbridge returned, and soon afterwards the dog-cart came to the door. My host and I mounted, Bainbridge took the reins, and we started off at a brisk pace.

"Matters get worse and worse," he said the moment we were alone. "If you don't clear things up to-night, Bell, I say frankly that I cannot imagine what will happen."

We entered the village, and as we rattled down the ill-paved streets I was greeted with curious glances on all sides. The people were standing about in groups, evidently talking about the tragedy and nothing else. Suddenly, as our trap bumped noisily over the paving-stones, a girl darted out of one of the houses and made frantic motions to Bainbridge to stop the horse. He pulled the mare nearly up on her haunches, and the girl came up to the side of the dog-cart.

"You have heard it?" she said, speaking eagerly and in a gasping voice. "The death which occurred this morning will clear Stephen Wynne, won't it, Mr. Bainbridge?—it will, you are sure, are you not?"

"It looks like it, Lucy, my poor girl," he answered. "But there, the whole thing is so terrible that I scarcely know what to think."

She was a pretty girl with dark eyes, and under ordinary circumstances must have had the vivacious expression of face and the brilliant complexion which so many of her country-women possess. But now her eyes were swollen with weep-ing and her complexion more or less disfigured by the agony she had gone through. She looked piteously at Bainbridge, her lips trembling. The next moment she burst into tears.

"Come away, Lucy," said a woman who had followed her out of the cottage; "Fie—for shame! don't trouble the gentle-men; come back and stay quiet."

"I can't, mother, I can't," said the unfortunate girl. "If they hang him, I'll go clean off my head. Oh, Mr. Bainbridge, do say that the second death has cleared him!"

"I have every hope that it will do so, Lucy," said Bainbridge, "but now don't keep us, there's a good girl; go back into the house. This gentleman has come down from London on purpose to look into the whole matter. I may have good news for you in the morning."

The girl raised her eyes to my face with a look of intense pleading. "Oh, I have been cruel and a fool, and I deserve everything," she gasped; "but, sir, for the love of Heaven, try to clear him."

I promised to do my best.

Bainbridge touched up the mare, she bounded forward, and Lucy disappeared into the cottage with her mother.

The next moment we drew up at the inn where the Inspector was waiting, and soon afterwards were bowling along between the high banks of the country lanes to the tunnel. It was a cold, still afternoon; the air was wonderfully keen, for a sharp frost had held the countryside in its grip for the last two days. The sun was just tipping the hills to westward when the trap pulled up at the top of the cutting. We hastily alighted, and the Inspector and I bade Bainbridge good-bye. He said that he only wished that he could stay with us for the night, assured us that little sleep would visit him, and that he would be back at the cutting at an early hour on the following morning; then the noise of his horse's feet was heard fainter and fainter as he drove back over the frost-bound roads. The Inspector and I ran along the little path to the wicket-gate in the fence, stamping our feet on the hard ground to restore circulation after our cold drive. The next moment we were looking down upon the scene of the mysterious deaths, and a weird and lonely place it looked. The tunnel was at one end of the rock cutting, the sides of which ran sheer down to the line for over a hundred and fifty feet. Above the tunnel's mouth the hills rose one upon the other. A more dreary place it would have been difficult to imagine. From a little clump of pines a delicate film of blue smoke rose straight up on the still air. This came from the chimney of the signal-box.

As we started to descend the precipitous path the Inspector sang out a cheery "Hullo!" The man on duty in the box immediately answered. His voice echoed and reverberated down the cutting, and the next moment he appeared at the door of the box. He told us that he would be with us immediately; but we called back to him to stay where he was, and the next instant the Inspector and I entered the box.

"The first thing to do," said Henderson the Inspector, "is to send a message down the line to announce our arrival."

This he did, and in a few moments a crawling goods train came panting up the cutting. After signalling her through we descended the wooden flight of steps which led from the box down to the line and walked along the metals towards the tunnel till we stood on the spot where poor Davidson had been found dead that morning. I examined the ground and all around it most carefully. Everything tallied exactly with the description I had received. There could be no possible way of approaching the spot except by going along the line, as the rocky sides of the cutting were inaccessible.

"It is a most extraordinary thing, sir," said the signalman whom we had come to relieve. "Davidson had neither mark nor sign on him—there he lay stone dead and cold, and not a bruise nowhere; but Pritchard had an awful wound at the back of the head. They said he got it by climbing the rocks—here, you can see the marks for yourself, sir. But now, is it likely that Pritchard would try to climb rocks like these, so steep as they are?"

"Certainly not," I replied.

"Then how do you account for the wound, sir?" asked the man with an anxious face.

"I cannot tell you at present," I answered.

"And you and Inspector Henderson are going to spend the night in the signal-box?"

"Yes."

A horrified expression crept over the signalman's face.

"God preserve you both," he said; "I wouldn't do it—not for fifty pounds. It's not the first time I have heard tell that Felwyn Tunnel is haunted. But, there, I won't say any more about that. It's a black business, and has given trouble enough. There's poor Wynne, the same thing as convicted of the murder of Pritchard; but now they say that Davidson's death will clear him. Davidson was as good a fellow as you would come across this side of the country; but for the matter of that, so was Pritchard. The whole thing is terrible—it upsets one, that it do, sir."

"I don't wonder at your feelings," I answered; "but now, see here, I want to make a most careful examination of everything. One of the theories is that Wynne crept down this rocky side and fractured Pritchard's skull. I believe such a feat to be impossible. On examining these rocks I see that a man might climb up the side of the tunnel as far as from eight to ten feet, utilising the sharp projections of rock for the purpose; but it would be out of the question for any man to come down the cutting. No; the only way Wynne could have approached Pritchard was by the line itself. But, after all, the real thing to discover is this," I continued: "what killed Davidson? Whatever caused his death is, beyond doubt, equally responsible for Pritchard's. I am now going into the tunnel."

Inspector Henderson went in with me. The place struck damp and chill. The walls were covered with green, evil-smelling fungi, and through the brickwork the moisture was oozing and had trickled down in long lines to the ground. Before us was nothing but dense darkness.

When we re-appeared the signalman was lighting the red lamp on the post, which stood about five feet from the ground just above the entrance to the tunnel.

"Is there plenty of oil?" asked the Inspector.

"Yes, sir, plenty," replied the man. "Is there anything more I can do for either of you gentlemen?" he asked, pausing, and evidently dying to be off.

"Nothing," answered Henderson; "I will wish you good-evening."

"Good-evening to you both," said the man. He made his way quickly up the path and was soon lost to sight.

Henderson and I then returned to the signal-box.

By this time it was nearly dark.

"How many trains pass in the night?" I asked of the Inspector.

"There's the 10.20 down express," he said, "it will pass here at about 10.40; then there's the 11.45 up, and then not another train till the 6.30 local to-morrow morning. We shan't have a very lively time," he added.

I approached the fire and bent over it, holding out my hands to try and get some warmth into them.

"It will take a good deal to persuade me to go down to the tunnel, whatever I may see there," said the man. "I don't think, Mr. Bell, I am a coward in any sense of the word, but there's something very uncanny about this place, right away from the rest of the world. I don't wonder one often hears of signalmen going mad in some of these lonely boxes. Have you any theory to account for these deaths, sir?"

"None at present," I replied.

"This second death puts the idea of Pritchard being murdered quite out of court," he continued.

"I am sure of it," I answered.

"And so am I, and that's one comfort," continued Henderson. "That poor girl, Lucy Ray, although she was to be blamed for her conduct, is much to be pitied now; and as to poor Wynne himself, he protests his innocence through thick and thin. He was a wild fellow, but not the sort to take the life of a fellow-creature. I saw the doctor this afternoon while I was waiting for you at the inn, Mr. Bell, and also the police-sergeant. They both say they do not know what Davidson died of. There was not the least sign of violence on the body."

"Well, I am as puzzled as the rest of you," I said. "I have one or two theories in my mind, but none of them will quite fit the situation."

The night was piercingly cold, and, although there was not a breath of wind, the keen and frosty air penetrated into the lonely signal-box. We spoke little, and both of us were doubt-less absorbed by our own thoughts and speculations. As to Henderson, he looked distinctly uncomfortable, and I cannot say that my own feelings were too pleasant. Never had I been given a tougher problem to solve, and never had I been so utterly at my wits' end for a solution.

Now and then the Inspector got up and went to the tele-graph instrument, which intermittently clicked away in its box. As he did so he made some casual remark and then sat down again. After the 10.40 had gone through, there followed a period of silence which seemed almost oppressive. All at once the stillness was broken by the whirr of the electric bell, which sounded so sharply in our ears that we both started. Henderson rose.

"That's the 11.45 coming," he said, and, going over to the three long levers, he pulled two of them down with a loud clang. The next moment, with a rush and a scream, the ex-press tore down the cutting, the carriage lights streamed past in a rapid flash, the ground trembled, a few sparks from the engine whirled up into the darkness, and the train plunged into the tunnel.

"And now," said Henderson, as he pushed back the levers, "not another train till daylight. My word, it is cold!"

It was intensely so. I piled some more wood on the fire and, turning up the collar of my heavy ulster, sat down at one end of the bench and leant my back against the wall. Henderson did likewise; we were neither of us inclined to speak. As a rule, whenever I have any night work to do, I am never troubled with sleepiness, but on this occasion I felt unaccountably drowsy. I soon perceived that Henderson was in the same condition.

"Are you sleepy?" I asked of him.

"Dead with it, sir," was his answer; "but there's no fear, I won't drop off."

I got up and went to the window of the box. I felt certain that if I sat still any longer I should be in a sound sleep. This would never do. Already it was becoming a matter of torture to keep my eyes open. I began to pace up and down; I opened the door of the box and went out on the little platform.

"What's the matter, sir?" inquired Henderson, jumping up with a start.

"I cannot keep awake," I said.

"Nor can I," he answered, "and yet I have spent nights and nights of my life in signal-boxes and never was the least bit drowsy; perhaps it's the cold."

"Perhaps it is," I said; "but I have been out on as freezing nights before, and——"

The man did not reply; he had sat down again; his head was nodding.

I was just about to go up to him and shake him, when it suddenly occurred to me that I might as well let him have his sleep out. I soon heard him snoring, and he presently fell forward in a heap on the floor. By dint of walking up and down, I managed to keep from dropping off myself, and in torture which I shall never be able to describe, the night wore itself away. At last, towards morning, I awoke Henderson.

"You have had a good nap," I said; "but never mind, I have been on guard and nothing has occurred."

"Good God! have I been asleep?" cried the man.

"Sound," I answered.

"Well, I never felt anything like it," he replied. "Don't you find the air very close, sir?"

"No," I said; "it is as fresh as possible; it must be the cold."

"I'll just go and have a look at the light at the tunnel," said the man; "it will rouse me."

He went on to the little platform, whilst I bent over the fire and began to build it up. Presently he returned with a scared look on his face. I could see by the light of the oil lamp which hung on the wall that he was trembling.

"Mr. Bell," he said, "I believe there is somebody or something down at the mouth of the tunnel now." As he spoke he clutched me by the arm. "Go and look," he said; "whoever it is, it has put out the light."

"Put out the light?" I cried. "Why, what's the time?"

Henderson pulled out his watch.

"Thank goodness, most of the night is gone," he said; "I didn't know it was so late, it is half-past five."

"Then the local is not due for an hour yet?" I said.

"No; but who should put out the light?" cried Henderson.

I went to the door, flung it open, and looked out. The dim outline of the tunnel was just visible looming through the darkness, but the red light was out.

"What the dickens does it mean, sir?" gasped the Inspector. "I know the lamp had plenty of oil in it. Can there be any one standing in front of it, do you think?"

We waited and watched for a few moments, but nothing stirred.

"Come along," I said, "let us go down together and see what it is."

"I don't believe I can do it, sir; I really don't!"

"Nonsense," I cried. "I shall go down alone if you won't accompany me. Just hand me my stick, will you?"

"For God's sake, be careful, Mr. Bell. Don't go down, whatever you do. I expect this is what happened before, and the poor fellows went down to see what it was and died there. There's some devilry at work, that's my belief."

"That is as it may be," I answered shortly; "but we certainly shall not find out by stopping here. My business is to get to the bottom of this, and I am going to do it. That there is danger of some sort, I have very little doubt; but danger or not, I am going down."

"If you'll be warned by me, sir, you'll just stay quietly here."

"I must go down and see the matter out," was my answer. "Now listen to me, Henderson. I see that you are alarmed, and I don't wonder. Just stay quietly where you are and watch, but if I call come at once. Don't delay a single instant. Remember I am putting my life into your hands. If I call 'Come,' just come to me as quick as you can, for I may want help. Give me that lantern."

He unhitched it from the wall, and taking it from him, I walked cautiously down the steps on to the line. I still felt curiously, unaccountably drowsy and heavy. I wondered at this, for the moment was such a critical one as to make almost any man wide awake. Holding the lamp high above my head, I walked rapidly along the line. I hardly knew what I expected to find. Cautiously along the metals I made my way, peering right and left until I was close to the fatal spot where the bodies had been found. An uncontrollable shudder passed over me. The next moment, to my horror, without the slightest warning, the light I was carrying went out, leaving me in total darkness. I started back, and stumbling against one of the loose boulders reeled against the wall and nearly fell. What was the matter with me? I could hardly stand. I felt giddy and faint, and a horrible sensation of great tightness seized me across the chest. A loud ringing noise sounded in my ears. Struggling madly for breath, and with the fear of impending death upon me, I turned and tried to run from a danger I could neither understand nor grapple with. But before I had taken two steps my legs gave way from under me, and uttering a loud cry I fell insensible to the ground.

* * * *

Out of an oblivion which, for all I knew, might have lasted for moments or centuries, a dawning consciousness came to me. I knew that I was lying on hard ground; that I was absolutely incapable of realising, nor had I the slightest inclination to discover, where I was. All I wanted was to lie quite still and undisturbed. Presently I opened my eyes.

Some one was bending over me and looking into my face.

"Thank God, he is not dead," I heard in whispered tones. Then, with a flash, memory returned to me.

"What has happened?" I asked.

"You may well ask that, sir," said the Inspector gravely. "It has been touch and go with you for the last quarter of an hour; and a near thing for me too."

I sat up and looked around me. Daylight was just beginning to break, and I saw that we were at the bottom of the steps that led up to the signal-box. My teeth were chattering with the cold and I was shivering like a man with ague.

"I am better now," I said; "just give me your hand."

I took his arm, and holding the rail with the other hand staggered up into the box and sat down on the bench.

"Yes, it has been a near shave," I said; "and a big price to pay for solving a mystery."

"Do you mean to say you know what it is?" asked Henderson eagerly.

"Yes," I answered, "I think I know now; but first tell me how long was I unconscious?"

"A good bit over half an hour, sir, I should think. As soon as I heard you call out I ran down as you told me, but before I got to you I nearly fainted. I never had such a horrible sensation in my life. I felt as weak as a baby, but I just managed to seize you by the arms and drag you along the line to the steps, and that was about all I could do."

"Well, I owe you my life," I said; "just hand me that brandy flask, I shall be the better for some of its contents."

I took a long pull. Just as I was laying the flask down Henderson started from my side.

"There," he cried, "the 6.30 is coming." The electric bell at the instrument suddenly began to ring. "Ought I to let her go through, sir?" he inquired.

"Certainly," I answered. "That is exactly what we want. Oh, she will be all right."

"No danger to her, sir?"

"None, none; let her go through."

He pulled the lever and the next moment the train tore through the cutting.

"Now I think it will be safe to go down again," I said, "I believe I shall be able to get to the bottom of this business."

Henderson stared at me aghast.

"Do you mean that you are going down again to the tunnel?" he gasped.

"Yes," I said; "give me those matches. You had better come too. I don't think there will be much danger now; and there is daylight, so we can see what we are about."

The man was very loth to obey me, but at last I managed to persuade him. We went down the line, walking slowly, and at this moment we both felt our courage revived by a broad and cheerful ray of sunshine.

"We must advance cautiously," I said, "and be ready to run back at a moment's notice."

"God knows, sir, I think we are running a great risk," panted poor Henderson; "and if that devil or whatever else it is should happen to be about—why, daylight or no day-light——"

"Nonsense! man," I interrupted; "if we are careful, no harm will happen to us now. Ah! and here we are!" We had reached the spot where I had fallen. "Just give me a match, Henderson."

He did so, and I immediately lit the lamp. Opening the glass of the lamp, I held it close to the ground and passed it to and fro. Suddenly the flame went out.

"Don't you understand now?" I said, looking up at the Inspector.

"No, I don't, sir," he replied with a bewildered expression.

Suddenly, before I could make an explanation, we both heard shouts from the top of the cutting, and looking up I saw Bainbridge hurrying down the path. He had come in the dog-cart to fetch us.

"Here's the mystery," I cried as he rushed up to us, "and a deadlier scheme of Dame Nature's to frighten and murder poor humanity I have never seen."

As I spoke I lit the lamp again and held it just above a tiny fissure in the rock. It was at once extinguished.

"What is it?" said Bainbridge, panting with excitement.

"Something that nearly finished *me*," I replied. "Why, this is a natural escape of choke damp. Carbonic acid gas—the deadliest gas imaginable, because it gives no warning of its presence, and it has no smell. It must have collected here during the hours of the night when no train was passing, and gradually rising put out the signal light. The constant rushing of the trains through the cutting all day would temporarily disperse it."

As I made this explanation Bainbridge stood like one electrified, while a curious expression of mingled relief and horror swept over Henderson's face.

"An escape of carbonic acid gas is not an uncommon phenomenon in volcanic districts," I continued, "as I take this to be; but it is odd what should have started it. It has sometimes been known to follow earthquake shocks, when there is a profound disturbance of the deep strata."

"It is strange that you should have said that," said Bainbridge, when he could find his voice.

"What do you mean?"

"Why, that about the earthquake. Don't you remember, Henderson," he added, turning to the Inspector, "we had felt a slight shock all over South Wales about three weeks back?"

"Then that, I think, explains it," I said. "It is evident that Pritchard really did climb the rocks in a frantic attempt to escape from the gas and fell back on to these boulders. The other man was cut down at once, before he had time to fly."

"But what is to happen now?" asked Bainbridge. "Will it go on for ever? How are we to stop it?"

"The fissure ought to be drenched with lime water, and then filled up; but all really depends on what is the size of the supply and also the depth. It is an extremely heavy gas, and would lie at the bottom of a cutting like water. I think there is more here just now than is good for us," I added.

"But how," continued Bainbridge, as we moved a few steps from the fatal spot, "do you account for the interval between the first death and the second?"

"The escape must have been intermittent. If wind blew down the cutting, as probably was the case before this frost set in, it would keep the gas so diluted that its effects would not be noticed. There was enough down here this morning, before that train came through, to poison an army. Indeed, if it had not been for Henderson's promptitude, there would have been another inquest—on myself."

I then related my own experience.

"Well, this clears Wynne, without doubt," said Bainbridge; "but alas! for the two poor fellows who were victims. Bell, the Lytton Vale Railway Company owe you unlimited thanks; you have doubtless saved many lives, and also the Company, for the line must have been closed if you had not made your valuable discovery. But now come home with me to breakfast. We can discuss all those matters later on."

THE EIGHT-MILE LOCK

It was in the August of 1889, when I was just arranging my annual holiday, that I received the following letter. I tore it open and read:—

"*Theodora* House-boat, GORING.

"Dear Mr. Bell,—

"Can you come down on Wednesday and stay with us for a week? The weather is glorious and the river looking its best. We are a gay party, and there will be plenty of fun going on.

"Yours very truly,

"HELENA RIDSDALE."

This was exactly what I wanted. I was fond of the river, and scarcely a summer passed that I did not spend at least a fortnight on the Thames. I could go for a week to the Ridsdales, and then start off on my own quiet holiday afterwards. I had known Lady Ridsdale since she was a girl, and I had no doubt my visit would prove a most enjoyable one. I replied immediately, accepting the invitation, and three days later arrived at Goring.

As the well-cushioned little punt, which had been sent to bring me across the river, drew up alongside the *Theodora*, the Countess came down from the deck to welcome me.

"I am so glad you could come, Mr. Bell," she said. "I was afraid you might be away on some of your extraordinary campaigns against the supernatural. This is Mr. Ralph Vyner; he is also, like yourself, devoted to science. I am sure you will find many interests in common."

A short, thickset, wiry little man, dressed in white flannels, who had been lolling in a deck chair, now came forward and shook hands with me.

"I know of you by reputation, Mr. Bell," he said, "and I have often hoped to have the pleasure of meeting you. I am sure we shall all be anxious to hear of some of your experiences. We are such an excessively frivolous party that we can easily afford to be leavened with a little serious element."

"But I don't mean to be serious in the least," I answered, laughing; "I have come here to enjoy myself, and intend to be as frivolous as the rest of you."

"You will have an opportunity this evening," said the Countess; "we are going to have a special band from town, and intend to have a moonlight dance on deck. Ah! here comes Charlie with the others," she added, shading her eyes and looking down the stream.

In a few moments a perfectly appointed little electric launch shot up, and my host with the rest of the party came on board. We shortly afterwards sat down to lunch, and a gayer and pleasanter set of people I have seldom met. In the afternoon we broke up into detachments, and Vyner and I went for a long pull up stream. I found him a pleasant fellow, ready to talk at any length not only about his own hobbies, but about the world at large. I discovered presently that he was a naval engineer of no small attainments.

When we returned to the house-boat, it was nearly time to prepare for dinner. Most of the ladies had already retired to their cabins. Lady Ridsdale was standing alone on deck. When she saw us both, she called to us to come to her side.

"This quite dazzles me," she said in a low, somewhat mysterious tone, "and I must show it to you. I know you at least, Mr. Vyner, will appreciate it."

As she spoke she took a small leather case out of her pocket—it was ornamented with a monogram, and opened with a catch. She pressed the lid, it flew up, and I saw, resting on a velvet bed, a glittering circlet of enormous diamonds. The Countess lifted them out, and slipped them over her slender wrist.

"They are some of the family diamonds," she said with excitement, "and of great value. Charlie is having all the jewels reset for me, but the rest are not ready yet. He has just brought this down from town. Is it not superb? Did you ever see such beauties?"

The diamonds flashed on her white wrist; she looked up at me with eyes almost as bright.

"I love beautiful stones," she said, "and I feel as if these were alive. Oh, do look at the rays of colour in them, as many as in the rainbow."

I congratulated Lady Ridsdale on possessing such a splendid ornament, and then glanced at Vyner, expecting him to say something.

The expression on his face startled me, and I was destined to remember it by-and-by. The ruddy look had completely left it, his eyes were half starting from his head. He peered close, and suddenly, without the slightest warning, stretched out his hand, and touched the diamonds as they glittered round Lady Ridsdale's wrist. She started back haughtily, then, recovering herself, took the bracelet off and put it into his hand.

"Charlie tells me," she said, "that this bracelet is worth from fifteen to twenty thousand pounds."

"You must take care of it," remarked Vyner; "don't let your maid see it, for instance."

"Oh, nonsense!" laughed Lady Ridsdale. "I would trust Louise as I would trust myself."

Soon afterwards we separated, and I went down to my little cabin to prepare for dinner. When we met in the dining saloon I noticed that Lady Ridsdale was wearing the diamond bracelet. Almost immediately after dinner the band came on board and the dancing began.

We kept up our festivities until two o'clock, and more than once, as she flashed past me, I could not help noticing the glittering circlet round her wrist. I considered myself a fair judge of precious stones, but had never seen any diamonds for size and brilliancy to equal these.

As Vyner and I happened to stand apart from the others he remarked upon them.

"It was imprudent of Ridsdale to bring those diamonds here," he said. "Suppose they are stolen?"

"Scarcely likely," I answered; "there are no thieves on board."

He gave an impatient movement.

"As far as we *know* there are not," he said slowly, "but one can never tell. The diamonds are of exceptional value, and it is not safe to expose ordinary folk to temptation. That small circlet means a fortune."

He sighed deeply, and when I spoke to him next did not answer me. Not long afterwards our gay party dispersed, and we retired to our respective cabins.

I went to mine and was quickly in bed. As a newly-arrived guest I was given a cabin on board, but several other members of the party were sleeping in tents on the shore. Vyner and Lord Ridsdale were amongst the latter number. Whether it was the narrowness of my bunk or the heat of the night, I cannot tell, but sleep I could not. Suddenly through my open window I heard voices from the shore near by. I could identify the speakers by their tones—one was my host, Lord Ridsdale, the other Ralph Vyner. Whatever formed the subject of discourse it was evidently far from amicable. However much averse I might feel to the situation, I was compelled to be an unwilling eavesdropper, for the voices rose, and I caught the following words from Vyner:

"Can you lend me five thousand pounds till the winter?"

"No, Vyner, I have told you so before, and the reason too. It is your own fault, and you must take the consequences."

"Do you mean that to be final?" asked Vyner.

"Yes."

"Very well, then I shall look after myself. Thank God, I have got brains if I have not money, and I shall not let the means interfere with the end."

"You can go to the devil for all I care," was the angry answer, "and, after what I know, I won't raise a finger to help you."

The speakers had evidently moved further off, for the last words I could not catch. But what little I heard by no means conduced to slumber. So Vyner, for all his jovial and easy manner, was in a fix for money, and Ridsdale knew something about him scarcely to his credit!

I kept thinking over this, and also recalling his words when he spoke of Lady Ridsdale's diamonds as representing a fortune. What did he mean by saying that he would not let the means interfere with the end? That brief sentence sounded very much like the outburst of a desperate man. I could not help heartily wishing that Lady Ridsdale's diamond circlet was back in London, and, just before I dropped to sleep, I made up my mind to speak to Ridsdale on the subject.

Towards morning I did doze off, but I was awakened by hearing my name called, and, starting up, I saw Ridsdale standing by my side. His face looked queer and excited.

"Wake up, Bell," he cried; "a terrible thing has happened."

"What is it?" I asked.

"My wife's bracelet is stolen."

Like a flash I thought of Vyner, and then as quickly I knew that I must be careful to give no voice to hastily-formed suspicions.

"I won't be a moment dressing, and then I'll join you," I said.

Ridsdale nodded and left my cabin.

In five minutes I was with him on deck. He then told me briefly what had happened.

"Helena most imprudently left the case on her dressing-table last night," he said, "and owing to the heat she kept the window open. Some one must have waded into the water in the dark and stolen it. Perhaps one of the bandsmen may have noticed the flashing of the diamonds onher wrist and returned to secure the bracelet—there's no saying. The only too palpable fact is that it is gone—it was valued at twenty thousand pounds!"

"Have you sent for the police?" I asked.

"Yes, and have also wired to Scotland Yard for one of their best detectives. Vyner took the telegram for me, and was to call at the police station on his way back. He is nearly as much upset as I am. This is a terrible loss. I feel fit to kill myself for my folly in bringing that valuable bracelet on board a house-boat."

"It was a little imprudent," I answered, "but you are sure to get it back."

"I hope so," he replied moodily.

Just then the punt with Vyner and a couple of policemen on board was seen rapidly approaching. Ridsdale went to meet them, and was soon in earnest conversation with the superintendent of police. The moment Vyner leapt on board he came to the part of the deck where I was standing.

"Ah, Bell," he cried, "what about my prognostications of last night?"

"They have been verified too soon," I answered. I gave him a quick glance. His eyes looked straight into mine.

"Have you any theory to account for the theft?" I asked.

"Yes, a very simple one. Owing to the heat of the evening the Countess slept with her window open. It was an easy matter to wade through the water, introduce a hand through the open window and purloin the diamonds."

"Without being seen by any occupants of the tents?" I queried.

"Certainly," he answered, speaking slowly and with thought.

"Then you believe the thief came from without?"

"I do."

"What about your warning to Lady Ridsdale yesterday evening not to trust her maid?"

I saw his eyes flash. It was the briefest of summer lightning that played in their depths. I knew that he longed to adopt the suggestion that I had on purpose thrown out, but dared not. That one look was enough for me. I had guessed his secret.

Before he could reply to my last remark Lord Ridsdale came up.

"What is to be done?" he said; "the police superintendent insists on our all, without respect of persons, being searched."

"There is nothing in that," I said; "it is the usual thing. I will be the first to submit to the examination."

The police went through their work thoroughly, and, of course, came across neither clue nor diamonds. We presently sat down to breakfast, but I don't think we any of us had much appetite. Lady Ridsdale's eyes were red with crying, and I could see that the loss had shaken both her nerve and fortitude. It was more or less of a relief when the post came in. Amongst the letters I found a telegram for myself. I knew what it meant before I opened it. It was from a man in a distant part of the country whom I had promised to assist in a matter of grave importance. I saw that it was necessary for me to return to town without delay. I was very loth to leave my host and hostess in their present dilemma, but there was no help for it, and soon after breakfast I took my leave. Ridsdale promised to write me if there was any news of the diamonds, and soon the circumstance passed more or less into the background of my brain, owing to the intense interest of the other matter which I had taken up. My work in the north was over, and I had returned to town, when I received a letter from Ridsdale.

"We are in a state of despair," he wrote; "we have had two detectives on board, and the police have moved heaven and earth to try and discover the bracelet—all in vain; not the slightest clue has been forthcoming. No one has worked harder for us than Vyner. He has a small place of his own further down the river, and comes up to see us almost daily. He has made all sorts of suggestions for the recovery of the diamonds, but hitherto they have led to nothing. In short, our one hope now turns upon you, Bell; you have done as difficult things as this before. Will you come and see us, and give us the benefit of your advice? If any man can solve this mystery, you are the person."

I wrote immediately to say that I would return to the *Theodora* on the following evening, and for the remainder of that day tried to the best of my ability to think out this most difficult problem. I felt morally certain that I could put my hand on the thief, but I had no real clue to work upon—nothing beyond a nameless suspicion. Strange as it may seem, I was moved by sentiment. I had spent some pleasant hours in Vyner's society—I had enjoyed his conversation; I had liked the man for himself. He had abilities above the average, of that I was certain—if he were proved guilty, I did not want to be the one to bring his crime home to him. So uncomfortable were my feelings that at last I made up my mind to take a somewhat bold step. This was neither more nor less than to go to see Vyner himself before visiting the house-boat. What I was to do and say when I got to him I was obliged to leave altogether to chance; but I had a feeling almost amounting to a certainty that by means of this visit I should ultimately return the bracelet to my friends the Ridsdales.

The next afternoon I found myself rowing slowly down the river, thinking what the issue of my visit to Vyner would be. It happened to be a perfect evening. The sun had just set. The long reach of river stretched away to the distant bend, where, through the gathering twilight, I could just see the white gates of the Eight-Mile Lock. Raising my voice, I sang out in a long-drawn, sonorous monotone the familiar cry of "Lock! lock! lock!" and, bending to the sculls, sent my little skiff flying down stream. The sturdy figure of old James Pegg, the lock-keeper, whom I had known for many years, instantly appeared on the bridge. One of the great gates slowly swung open, and, shipping my sculls, I shot in, and called out a cheery good-evening to my old friend.

"Mr. Bell!" exclaimed the old fellow, hurrying along the edge of the lock. "Well, I never! I did not see it was you at first, and yet I ought to have known that long, swinging stroke of yours. You are the last person I expected to see. I was half afraid it might be some one else, although I don't know that I was expecting any one in particular. Excuse me, sir, but was it you called out 'Lock' just now?"

"Of course it was," I answered, laughing. "I'm in the deuce of a hurry to-night, Jimmy, as I want to get on to Wotton before dark. Look sharp, will you, and let me down."

"All right, sir—but you did frighten me just now. I wish you hadn't called out like that!"

As I glanced up at him, I was surprised to see that his usually ruddy, round face was as white as a sheet, and he was breathing quickly.

"Why, what on earth is the matter, Jimmy?" I cried; "how can I have frightened you?"

"Oh, it's nothing, sir; I suppose I'm an old fool," he faltered, smiling. "I don't know what's the matter with me, sir—I'm all of a tremble. The fact is, something happened here last night, and I don't seem to have got over it. You know, I am all by myself here now, sir, and a lonely place it is."

"Something happened?" I said; "not an accident, I hope?"

"No, sir, no accident that I know of, and yet I have been half expecting one to occur all day, and I have been that weak I could hardly wind up the sluices. I am getting old now, and I'm not the man I was; but I'm right glad to see you, Mr. Bell, that I am."

He kept pausing as he spoke, and now and then glanced up the river, as if expecting to see a boat coming round the bend every moment. I was much puzzled by his extraordinary manner. I knew him to be a steady man, and one whose services were much valued by the Conservancy; but it needed only a glance now to show that there was something very much amiss with him.

The darkness was increasing every moment, and, being anxious to get on as soon as possible, I was just going to tell him again to hurry up with the sluices, when he bent down close to me, and said,—

"Would you mind stepping out for a moment, sir, if you can spare the time? I wish to speak to you, sir. I'd be most grateful if you would wait a minute or two."

"Certainly, Jimmy," I answered, hauling myself to the side with the boat-hook, and getting out. "Is there anything I can do for you? I am afraid you are not well. I never saw you like this before."

"No, sir; and I never felt like it before, that I can remember. Something happened here last night that has taken all the nerve out of me, and I want to tell you what it was. I know you are so clever, Mr. Bell, and I have heard about your doings up at Wallinghurst last autumn, when you cleared up the Manor House ghost, and got old Monkford six months."

"Well, fire away," I said, filling my pipe, and wondering what was coming.

"It is this way, sir," he began. "Last night after I had had my supper I thought I'd like a stroll and a quiet smoke along the towing path before turning in. I did not expect any more boats, as it was getting on for ten o'clock. I walked about three-quarters of a mile, and was just going to turn round, when I saw a light down on the surface of the water in mid-stream. It was pretty dark, for the moon was not up yet, and there was a thick white mist rising from the water. I thought it must be some one in a canoe at first, so I waited a bit and watched. Then it suddenly disappeared, and the next instant I saw it again about a hundred yards or so higher up the stream, but only for a second, and then it went out. It fairly puzzled me to know what it could be, as I had never seen anything like it before. I felt sure it wasn't any sort of craft, but I had heard of strange lights being seen at times on the water—what they call jack-o'-lanterns, I believe, sir. I reckoned it might be one of them, but I thought I'd get back to the lock, so that, if it was a canoe, I could let it through. However, nothing came of it, and I waited and watched, and worried all the evening about it, but couldn't come to any sort of idea, so I went to bed. Well, about one o'clock this morning I suddenly woke up and thought I could hear some one a long way off calling exactly as you did just now, 'Lock! lock! lock!' but it sounded ever so far away.

"'It's some of those theatre people coming back to the *Will-o'-the-Wisp* house-boat,' I said to myself, 'and I'm not going to turn out for them.' The lock was full at the time, so I thought I would just let them work it for themselves. I waited a bit, expecting to hear them every minute come up, singing and swearing as they do, but they never came, and I was just dropping off when I heard the call again. It was not an ordinary sort of voice, but a long, wailing cry, just as if some one was in trouble or drowning. 'Hi! hi! Lock! lo-oock!' it went.

"I got up then and went out. The moon was up now and quite bright, and the mist had cleared off, so I went to the bridge on the upper gates and looked up stream. This is where I was standing, sir, just as we are standing now. I could see right up to the bend, and there was not the sign of a boat. I stood straining my eyes, expecting to see a boat come round every moment, when I heard the cry again, and this time it sounded not fifty yards up stream. I could not make it out at all, so I shouted out as loud as I could, 'Who are you? What's the matter?' but there was no answer; and then suddenly, the next instant, close below me, from *inside* the lock this time, just here, came a shout, piercing, shrill, and loud, 'Open the lock, quick, quick! Open the lock!'

"I tell you, sir, my heart seemed to stand dead still, and I nearly fell back over the bridge. I wheeled round sharp, but there was nothing in the lock, that I'll swear to my dying day—for I could see all over it, and nothing could have got in there without passing me. The moon was quite bright, and I could see all round it. Without knowing what I was doing, I rushed down like mad to the lower gates, and began to wind up one of the sluices, and then I stood there and waited, but nothing came. As the lock emptied I looked down, but there was no sign of anything anywhere, so I let down the sluice without opening the gates, and then filled up the lock again. I stood by the post, hardly daring to move, when, about half-past five, thank God, I heard the whistle of a tug, and, after seeing her through, it was broad daylight.

"That's the whole story, sir, and how I'm going to live through the night again I don't know. It was a spirit if ever there was one in the world. It's a warning to me, sir; and what's going to happen I don't know."

"Well, Jimmy," I answered, "it certainly is a most extraordinary story, and if I didn't know you as well as I do, I should say you had taken something more than a smoke before you turned in last night."

"I never touch a drop, sir, except when I go into Farley and have a glass of beer, but I have not been there for more than a week now."

I confess that Jimmy's story had left a most unpleasant impression on me. I had little doubt that the whole thing was some strange subjective hallucination, but for a weird and ghostly experience it certainly beat most of the tales I had ever heard. I thought for a moment—it was now quite dark, and I felt little inclined to go on to Wotton. My keenest interests were awakened.

"Look here," I said, "what do you say if I stay here to-night? Can you give me a shake-down of any sort?"

"That I will, sir, and right gladly, and thank God if you will but stay with me. If I was alone here again, and heard that voice, I believe it would kill me. I'll tie up your boat outside, and bring your things in, and then we'll have supper. I'll feel a new man with you staying here, sir."

In a few minutes we were both inside old Jimmy's cosy quarters. His whole bearing seemed to have changed suddenly, and he ran about with alacrity, getting supper ready, and seeming quite like himself again. During the whole evening he kept harping at intervals on the subject of the mysterious voice, but we heard no sound whatever, and I felt more and more certain that the whole thing was due to hallucination on the part of the old man. At eleven o'clock a skiff came up through the lock, and almost immediately afterwards I bade Jimmy good-night and went into the little room he had prepared for me.

I went quickly to bed, and, tired after my long pull, despite the originality of the situation, fell fast asleep. Suddenly I awoke—some one was bending over me and calling me by my name. I leapt up, and, not realising where I was for the moment, but with a sort of dim idea that I was engaged in some exposure, instinctively seized the man roughly by the throat. In a moment I remembered everything, and quickly released my grip of poor old Jimmy, who was gurgling and gasping with horror. I burst out laughing at my mistake, and begged his pardon for treating him so roughly.

"It is all right, sir," he panted. "I hope I didn't frighten you, but I have heard it again, not five minutes ago."

"The deuce you have," I said, striking a match and looking at my watch.

It was nearly two o'clock, and before the minute was up I heard distinctly a cry, as if from some great distance, of "Lock, lock, lock!" and then all was silence again.

"Did you hear it, sir?" whispered the old man, clutching me by the arm with a trembling hand.

"Yes, I heard it," I said. "Don't you be frightened, Jimmy; just wait till I get my clothes on; I am going to see this thing through."

"Be careful, sir; for God's sake, be careful," he whispered.

"All right," I said, slipping on some things. "Just get me a good strong boat-hook, and don't make too much noise. If this mystery is flesh and blood I'll get to the bottom of it somehow. You stay here; and if I call, come out."

I took the thick, short boat-hook which he had brought me and, softly unlatching the door, went out.

The moon was now riding high overhead and casting black fantastic shadows across the little white cottage. All my senses were on the keenest alert, my ears were pricked up for the slightest sound. I crept softly to the bridge on the upper gate which was open. I looked up stream and thought I could see some little ripples on the surface of the water as if a swift boat had just passed down, but there was no sign of any craft whatever to be seen. It was intensely still, and no sound broke the silence save the intermittent croaking of some bull-frogs in the dark shadows of the pollards on the further bank. Behind me could also be heard the gurgling twinkle of the overflow through the chinks of the lower gate.

I stood quite still, gripping the boat-hook in my hand, and looking right and left, straining my eyes for the slightest movement of anything around, when suddenly, close below me from the water, inside the lock, came a loud cry—

"Open the lock, for God's sake, open the lock!"

I started back, feeling my hair rise and stiffen. The sound echoed and reverberated through the silent night, and then died away; but before it had done so I had sprung to the great beam and closed the upper gate. As I did so I caught sight of the old man trembling and shaking at the door of the cottage. I called to him to go and watch the upper gate, and, racing down to the lower ones, wound up one of the sluices with a few pulls, so as to let out the water with as little escape room as possible. I knew by this means if there were any creature of tangible form in the water we must find it when the lock was emptied, as its escape was cut off.

Each of the following minutes seemed stretched into a lifetime as, with eyes riveted on the dark water in the lock, I watched its gradual descent. I hardly dared to think of what I expected to see rise to the surface any moment. Would the lock never empty? Down, down sank the level, and still I saw nothing. A long, misshapen arm of black cloud was slowly stretching itself across the moon.

Hark! there was something moving about down in the well of darkness below me, and as I stood and watched I saw that the water was uncovering a long, black mass and that something ran slowly out of the water and began to clamber up the slimy, slippery beams. What in the name of heaven could it be? By the uncertain light I could only see its dim outline; it seemed to have an enormous bulbous head and dripping, glistening body. The sound of a rapid patter up the tow-path told me that the old man had seen it and was running for his life.

I rushed down to where the thing was, and as its great head appeared above the edge, with all my force struck it a terrific blow with the boat-hook. The weapon flew into splinters in my hand, and the next moment the creature had leapt up beside me and dashed me to the ground with almost superhuman force. I was up and on to it again in a second, and as I caught and closed with it saw that I had at least to deal with a human being, and that what he lacked in stature he more than made up for in strength. The struggle that ensued was desperate and furious. The covering to his head that had splintered the boat-hook was, I saw, a sort of helmet, completely protecting the head from any blow, and the body was cased in a slippery, closely fitting garment that kept eluding my grasp. To and fro we swayed and wrestled, and for a moment I thought I had met my match till, suddenly freeing my right arm, I got in a smashing blow in the region of the heart. The creature uttered a cry of pain and fell headlong to the ground.

Old Jimmy Pegg had hurried back as soon as he heard our struggles and knew that he was not dealing with a being of another world. He ran up eagerly to me.

"Here's your ghost, you old coward!" I panted; "he has got the hardest bone and muscle I ever felt in a ghost yet. I am not used to fighting men in helmets, and he is as slippery as an eel, but I hope to goodness I have not done more than knock the wind out of him. He is a specimen I should rather like to take alive. Catch hold of his feet and we'll get him inside and see who he is."

Between us we carried the prostrate figure inside the cottage and laid him down like a log on the floor. He never moved nor uttered a sound, and I was afraid at first that I had finished him for good and all. I next knelt down and proceeded to unfasten the helmet, which, from its appearance, was something like the kind used by divers, while the old man brought the lantern close to his face. At the first glance I knew in an instant that I had seen the face before, and the next second recognised, to my utter astonishment and horror, that it belonged to Ralph Vyner.

For the moment I was completely dumbfounded, and gazed at the man without speaking. It was obvious that he had only fainted from the blow, for I could see that he was breathing, and in a few minutes he opened his eyes and fixed them on me with a dull and vacant stare. Then he seemed to recall the situation, though he evidently did not recognise me.

"Let me go," he cried, making an effort to rise. "My God! you have killed me." He pressed his hand to his side and fell back again: his face was contorted as if in great pain.

There was obviously only one thing to be done, and that was to send for medical assistance at once. It was clear that the man was badly injured, but to what extent I could not determine. It was impossible to extract the slightest further communication from him—he lay quite still, groaning from time to time.

I told Jimmy to go off at once to Farley and bring the doctor. I scribbled a few directions on a piece of paper.

The old man hurried out of the cottage, but in less than a minute he was back again in great excitement.

"Look here, sir, what I have just picked up," he said; "it's something he has dropped, I reckon."

As Jimmy spoke he held out a square leather case: there was a monogram on it. I took it in my hand and pressed the lid; it flew open, and inside, resting on its velvet bed, lay the glittering circlet of diamonds. I held Lady Ridsdale's lost bracelet in my hand. All my suspicions were confirmed: Vyner was the thief.

Without saying a word I shut the box and despatched the old man at once for the doctor, bidding him go as fast as he could. Then I sat down by the prostrate man and waited. I knew that Jimmy could not be back for at least two hours. The grey dawn was beginning to steal in through the little latticed window when Vyner moved, opened his eyes and looked at me. He started as his eyes fell on the case.

"You are Mr. Bell," he said slowly. "Ridsdale told me that you were coming to the *Theodora* on purpose to discover the mystery of the lost diamonds. You didn't know that I should give you an opportunity of discovering the truth even before you arrived at the house-boat. Bend down close to me—you have injured me; I may not recover; hear what I have to say."

I bent over him, prepared to listen to his words, which came out slowly.

"I am a forger and a desperate man. Three weeks ago I forged one of Ridsdale's cheques and lessened my friend's balance to the tune of five thousand pounds. He and his wife were old friends of mine, but I wanted the money desperately, and was impervious to sentiment or anything else. On that first day when you met me, although I seemed cheery enough, I was fit to kill myself. I had hoped to be able to restore the stolen money long before Ridsdale was likely to miss it. But this hope had failed. I saw no loophole of escape, and the day of reckoning could not be far off. What devil prompted Ridsdale to bring those diamonds on board, Heaven only knows. The moment I saw them they fascinated me and I knew I should have a try for them. All during that evening's festivity I could think of nothing else. I made up my mind to secure them by hook or by crook. Before we retired for the night, however, I thought I would give Ridsdale a chance. I asked him if he would lend me the exact sum I had already stolen from him, five thousand pounds, but he had heard rumours to my discredit and refused point-blank. I hated him for it. I went into my tent under the pretence of lying down, but in reality to concoct and, if possible, carry out my plot. I waited until the quietest hour before dawn, then I slipped out of my tent, waded into the water, approached the open window of the Countess's cabin, thrust in my hand, took out the case, and, going down the river about a quarter of a mile, threw the diamonds into the middle of the stream. I marked well the place where they sank; I then returned to my tent and went to bed.

"You know what occurred the following morning. I neither feared Ridsdale nor his wife, but you, Bell, gave me a considerable amount of uneasiness. I felt certain that in an evil moment on the night before I had given you a clue. To a man of your ability the slightest clue was all-sufficient. I felt that I must take the bull by the horns and find out whether you suspected me or not. I talked to you, and guessed by the tone of your remarks that you had your suspicions. My relief was immense when that telegram arrived which hurried you away from the *Theodora*. On the following day I returned to my own little place on the banks of the river four miles below this lock. I knew it was necessary for me to remain quiet for a time, but all the same my plans were clearly made, and I only waited until the first excitement of the loss had subsided and the police and detectives were off their guard. In the meantime I went to see Ridsdale almost daily, and suggested many expedients for securing the thief and getting hold of the right clue. If he ever suspected me, which I don't for a moment suppose, I certainly put him off the scent. My intention was to take the diamonds out of the country, sell them for all that I could get, then return the five thousand pounds which I had stolen from his bank, and leave England for ever. As a forger I should be followed to the world's end, but as the possessor of stolen diamonds I felt myself practically safe. My scheme was too cleverly worked out to give the ordinary detective a chance of discovering me.

"Two days ago I had a letter from Ridsdale in which he told me that he intended to put the matter into your hands. Now this was by no means to my mind, for you, Bell, happened to be the one man in the world whom I really dreaded. I saw that I must no longer lose time. Under my little boat-house I had a small submarine boat which I had lately finished, more as a hobby than anything else. I had begun it years ago in my odd moments on a model I had seen of a torpedo used in the American War. My boat is now in the lock outside, and you will see for yourself what ingenuity was needed to construct such a thing. On the night before the one which has just passed, I got it ready, and, as soon as it was dark, started off in it to recover the diamonds. I got through the lock easily by going in under the water with a barge, but when I reached the spot where I had sunk the diamonds, found to my dismay that my electric light would not work. There was no help for it—I could not find the bracelet without the aid of the light, and was bound to return home to repair the lamp. This delay was fraught with danger, but there was no help for it. My difficulty now was to get back through the lock; for though I waited for quite three hours no boats came along. I saw the upper gates were open, but how to get through the lower ones I could not conceive. I felt sure that my only chance was to frighten the lock-keeper, and get him to open the sluices, for I knew I could pass through them unobserved if they were open, as I had done once before.

"In my diver's helmet was a thick glass face-piece. This had an opening, closed by a cap, which could be unscrewed, and through which I could breathe when above water, and also through which my voice would come, causing a peculiar hollowness which I guessed would have a very startling effect, especially as I myself would be quite invisible. I got into the lock, and shouted to Pegg. I succeeded in frightening him; he hurried to do what I ordered. He wound up the lower sluice, I shot through under water, and so got back unseen. All yesterday I hesitated about trying the experiment again, the risk was so great; but I knew that Ridsdale was certain to see his bank-book soon, that my forgery was in imminent danger of being discovered, also that you, Bell, were coming upon the scene.

"Yes, at any risk, I must now go on.

"I repaired my light, and again last night passed through the lock on my way up, by simply waiting for another boat. As a matter of fact, I passed up through this lock under a skiff about eleven o'clock. My light was now all right, I found the diamond case easily, and turned to pass down the stream by the same method as before. If you had not been here I should have succeeded, and should have been safe, but now it is all up."

He paused, and his breath came quickly.

"I doubt if I shall recover," he said in a feeble voice.

"I hope you will," I replied; "and hark! I think I hear the doctor's steps."

I was right, for a moment or two later old Jimmy Pegg and Dr. Simmons entered the cottage. While the doctor was examining the patient and talking to him, I went out with Jimmy to have a look at the submarine boat. By fixing a rope round it we managed to haul it up, and then proceeded to examine it. It certainly was the most wonderful piece of ingenious engineering I had ever seen. The boat was in the shape of an enormous cigar, and was made of aluminium. It was seven feet long, and had a circular beam of sixteen inches. At the pointed end, close to where the occupant's feet would be, was an air chamber capable of being filled or emptied at will by means of a compressed air cylinder, enabling the man to rise or sink whenever he wished to. Inside, the boat was lined with flat chambers of compressed air for breathing purposes, which were governed by a valve. It was also provided with a small accumulator and electric motor which drove the tiny propeller astern. The helmet which the man wore fitted around the opening at the head end.

After examining the boat it was easy to see how Vyner had escaped through the lock the night before I arrived, as this submarine wonder of ingenuity would be able to shoot through the sluice gate under water, when the sluice was raised to empty the lock.

After exchanging a few remarks with Jimmy, I returned to the cottage to learn the doctor's verdict.

It was grave, but not despairing. The patient could not be moved for a day or two. He was, in Dr. Simmons's opinion, suffering more from shock than anything else. If he remained perfectly quiet, he would in all probability recover; if he were disturbed, the consequences might be serious.

An hour afterwards I found myself on my way up stream sculling as fast as I could in the direction of the *Theodora*. I arrived there at an early hour, and put the case which contained the diamonds into Lady Ridsdale's hands.

I shall never forget the astonishment of Ridsdale and his wife when I told my strange tale. The Countess burst into tears, and Ridsdale was terribly agitated.

"I have known Vyner from a boy, and so has my wife," he exclaimed. "Of course, this proves him to be an unmitigated scoundrel, but I cannot be the one to bring him to justice."

"Oh, no, Charlie, whatever happens we must forgive him," said Lady Ridsdale, looking up with a white face.

I had nothing to say to this, it was not my affair. Unwittingly I had been the means of restoring to the Ridsdales their lost bracelet; they must act as they thought well with regard to the thief.

As a matter of fact, Vyner did escape the full penalty of his crime. Having got back the diamonds Lord Ridsdale would not prosecute. On the contrary, he helped the broken-down man to leave the country. From the view of pure justice he was, of course, wrong, but I could not help being glad.

As an example of what a desperate man will do, I think it would be difficult to beat Vyner's story. The originality and magnitude of the conception, the daring which enabled the man, single-handed, to do his own dredging in a submarine boat in one of the reaches of the Thames have seldom been equalled.

As I thought over the whole scheme, my only regret was that such ability should not have been devoted to nobler ends.

HOW SIVA SPOKE

During the summer of the past year a medical friend of mine sent me an invitation to dine with him and two of his fellow-craftsmen at the Welcome Club at the Earl's Court Exhibition. One of our party was a certain Dr. Laurier, a young man of considerable ability, whose special attention had been directed to mental diseases. He was, indeed, a noted authority on this subject, and had just completed an appointment at one of the large London asylums. During dinner he entertained us with a few of his late experiences—

"I assure you, Mr. Bell," he said, "there is absolutely no limit to the vagaries of the human mind. At the present moment a most grotesque and painful form of mental disease has come under my notice. The patient is not a pauper, but a gentleman of good standing and means. He is unmarried, and owns a lovely place in the country. He spent the early years of his life in India, and when there the craze began which now assumes the magnitude of a monomania."

"Pray let me hear about him, if your professional etiquette allows you to talk on the subject," I answered.

"I will certainly tell you what I can," he replied. "I have known the man for years, having met him in town on several occasions. Last week his nephew came to see me, and spoke seriously with regard to his uncle's state of mind. His great craze for years has been spiritualism, theosophy, and mahatmas, with all their attendant hocus-pocus. He firmly believes in his power to call up spirits from the vasty deep, and holds many extraordinary séances."

"But surely such a craze is not sufficient to prove insanity!" I said. "Hundreds of people believe in such manifestations at the present day."

"I know that well, and perfectly harmless such crazes are so long as the victims confine their beliefs to spirit-rapping, table-turning, and humbug of that sort; but when their convictions lead them to commit actions which compromise serious interests, and when, as in this case, there is a possibility of life itself being in danger, it is time they should be looked after."

"What is the particular nature of your friend's delusion?" I asked.

"This. He is practically a Brahmin, having been deeply imbued with the peculiar doctrines of Brahminism when in India. Amongst his friends in the East was a Brahmin of high degree in whose house were three idols, representing the Hindu Trinity—Vishnu, Brahma, and Siva. By some means which have never been explained to me, my friend managed to get possession of Siva, and brought the idol home. He placed it in a gallery which he has in his house, believing from the first that it possessed mystical properties which it was his duty to fathom. The nephew now tells me that he has brought his craze to such a pass that he firmly believes that Siva speaks to him in Hindustanee. The unhappy man kneels nightly at the altar in front of the idol, receiving, as he imagines, directions from him. The consequence is that he does all sorts of mad and extraordinary things, spending his large fortune lavishly in the decoration of this hideous monster, buying pearls, rubies, and even diamonds for the purpose, and really being, as he imagines, guided by it in the disposition of his life and property. He has a young niece residing with him, to whom he has always been very much attached; but of late he has been cruel to her, banishing her from his presence, refusing her his sympathy, and has even gone to the length of threatening to take her life, saying quite openly that Siva informs him night after night of her treachery towards him. Now the nephew is engaged to this girl, and is naturally anxious about her; but, say what he will, nothing will induce her to turn against her uncle, to whom she is deeply attached. She denies that he threatens her life, although the nephew declares that he did so in his own presence. Under such circumstances, her friends are, naturally, most anxious about her, and feel it their duty to get a medical opinion with regard to the uncle. I am going down to his place to-morrow, and shall there meet his regular medical attendant in consultation."

"And then, I suppose, certify as to his insanity?" I answered.

"Doubtless; that is, if we come to the conclusion that the man is really insane."

"What an awful responsibility is reposed in you doctors!" I said. "Think what it means to condemn a man to a lunatic asylum. In the hands of the unscrupulous such a power is terrible."

Dr. Laurier knitted his brows, and looked keenly at me.

"What do you mean?" he said in a curious tone. "Of course mistakes are made now and then, but not, I believe, often. To act in good faith and exercise reasonable care are the two requisites of the law."

"Of course," I replied, "there are great difficulties on both sides of this momentous question; but if I belonged to the profession, I can frankly say that nothing would induce me to sign a certificate of lunacy."

A few moments afterwards we all rose and strolled about the grounds. As we were parting at the exit gates I called Dr. Laurier aside.

"The love of mystery is to me a ruling passion," I said. "Will you excuse the great liberty I take when I ask you to let me know the result of your visit of to-morrow? I am immensely interested in your spiritualist patient."

As I spoke I scribbled my address on a card and handed it to him, half expecting that he would resent my intrusiveness. A smile flitted across his clever face, and he stood looking at me for a moment under the glare of the great arc lights.

"I will certainly give you the result of my visit, as you are so much interested," he replied. "Good-night."

We got into our respective hansoms, and drove off in different directions.

I had much to do, and soon forgot both Dr. Laurier and his patient; therefore, on the following Monday, when he was ushered into my presence, my surprise was great.

"I have come to fulfil my promise," he began. "I am here not only to satisfy your curiosity about my patient, but also to ask your advice. The fact is the matter has, I think, now merged more into your domain than mine."

"Pray tell me what has happened," I asked.

"That is what I am about to do; but first I must ensure your absolute confidence and secrecy, for my professional reputation may be seriously compromised if it is known that I consulted you."

I gave him the assurance, and he proceeded:—

"My patient's name is Edward Thesiger; he lives in a place called The Hynde, in Somersetshire. I went down as I had arranged, and was met at the station by his nephew, Jasper Bagwell. Bagwell is a thin, anxious-looking man of about five-and-thirty. He drove me over to The Hynde, and I was there met by Thesiger's own physician, Dr. Dalton. Dalton and I each made a separate examination of the patient, and came to the conclusion that he was undoubtedly queer.

"In the course of the afternoon we were all wandering round the grounds, when we were joined by the young girl to whom Bagwell is engaged. When she saw me she gave me a very eager glance, and soon attached herself to my side.

"'I want to speak to you, Dr. Laurier,' she said in a low voice.

"I managed to drop behind in order to give her an opportunity.

"'I know what you have come about,' she said. 'What do you think of my uncle's case?'

"'I am not prepared to hazard an opinion,' I replied.

"'Well, please listen to something I have got to say. Jasper Bagwell has his own reasons for what he tells you. You do very wrong to listen to him. Uncle Edward is queer, I grant, with regard to the idol Siva, that is because he is in reality a

Brahmin; but if you sign a certificate to the effect that he is mad, you will be making a very terrible mistake.'

"As she spoke her lips trembled, and tears filled her eyes.

"'I am terribly unhappy about it all,' she continued.

"I looked at her earnestly, then I said in a low voice:

"'Forgive me if I reply to you as plainly as you have just spoken to me. You arouse my surprise when you speak as you do of Mr. Bagwell. Is it not the case that you are engaged to marry him?'

"She gave a visible start.

"'It is the case,' she answered slowly. Then she continued, speaking with great emphasis, 'I only marry my cousin because it is the one—the one chance of saving Uncle Edward.'

"'What do you mean?' I asked in astonishment.

"'I wish I could tell you, but I dare not. I am a very miserable girl. There is foul play somewhere, of that I am convinced. Oh, believe me! won't you believe me?'

"To these extraordinary words I made a somewhat dubious reply, and she soon left me, to walk by her uncle's side.

"Late that evening I was alone with the patient, and he then confided to me much which he had withheld at first. He spoke about the years he had spent in India, and in especial alluded to the Brahmin religion. He told me also that he now possesses the idol Siva, and has set it up in a marble gallery where he can hold his spiritualistic séances. Bending forward as he spoke, and fixing me with his intelligent and yet strange glance, he said solemnly, and with an appearance of perfect truth on his face, that by certain incenses and secret incantations he could make the idol speak to him in Hindustanee. He said further that he felt himself completely dominated by it, and was bound to obey all its dictates. As he said the latter words his face grew white to the lips.

"'Siva is exigent in his demands,' he said slowly—'exigent and terrible. But come, I will take you into the gallery, and you shall see him for yourself.'

"I went gladly. We had to go through a long conservatory which opened out of the dining-room; from there we entered an oval-shaped room. Thesiger brought me straight up to the idol. It was placed upon a pedestal. It is a hideous monster made of wood, and has five heads; in its hand it holds a trident. I could hardly refrain from smiling when I first saw it. It was difficult to believe that any man, sane or insane, could hold faith in such a monstrosity. My object, however, was to draw the poor mad fellow out, and I begged of him to take what steps he considered necessary in order to induce the creature to speak. He willingly obeyed my desire, and with great solemnity went through elaborate operations; then, turning the lamp very low, knelt at the altar in front of the idol and began to address it. He waited for its replies, which were, of course, inaudible, and then continued speaking again. After some moments spent in this way he declared solemnly that it had replied to him, and practically called me a liar when I said I had not heard it.

"When he turned up the lamp at the end of this strange scene, I noticed for the first time that the idol was decorated with precious stones of extraordinary value. To leave such valuables in a room with an unlocked door was in itself a symptom of insanity, and when I parted with Thesiger for the night I had not the least doubt that my unfortunate host was really insane. All the same, I had a curious unwillingness with regard to signing the certificate. Bagwell eagerly asked me if I did not intend to sign. To his astonishment, I replied in the negative. I said that the case was a very peculiar one, and that it would be necessary for me to pay a second visit to the patient before I could take this extreme step. He was, I could see, intensely annoyed, but I remained firm."

Laurier stopped speaking and looked me full in the face.

"Well?" I asked.

"I have come to consult with you over the matter. You remember what you said about the responsibility of signing such certificates! It is on account of those words I have come to you."

"Well, Dr. Laurier," I answered, "I shall of course be happy to do anything I can to help you, but I must frankly confess that I fail to see exactly on what point I can be of service. I know little about disease in general, and nothing about mental diseases in particular. Miss Thesiger seems to think that there is foul play; but have you any suspicions on your own account?"

"I have no proofs, but, all the same, I do suspect foul play, although, perhaps, I have no right to say so."

"Then what do you want me to do?" I asked.

"This," he answered. "Will you come down with me to Somersetshire as my friend, and in the *rôle* of a great spiritualist? Thesiger will be only too delighted to meet some one of his own way of thinking. Will you come?"

I thought for a moment—it was not a *rôle* I cared to assume, but the case was peculiar, and might possibly lie within my province. I eventually agreed to accompany Laurier into Somersetshire, and, as a matter of fact, went down with him the next day. He had telegraphed our arrival to The Hynde, and a hearty invitation was accorded to me.

As we were driving through the grounds late the following afternoon we were met by a tall girl, who was accompanied by two thoroughbred retrievers.

"Here is Miss Thesiger," said Laurier. He called to the driver to stop, and jumping down, went to her side. I accompanied him.

"Miss Thesiger," said Laurier, "let me introduce my friend, Mr. John Bell."

She looked me full in the face, then her grey eyes seemed to lighten with momentary pleasure, and she held out her hand.

"What have you come back for?" she asked the next moment, turning to Laurier.

"To see your uncle."

"Are you to meet Dr. Dalton?" her lips trembled.

"I believe so. I assure you, Miss Thesiger, I have come with no sinister design." Laurier smiled as he spoke. "On the contrary, I am here to-day in order, if possible, to get at the truth. There is no one who can help me better than this gentleman."

"Then you do suspect foul play?" she said, her eyes lighting up with sudden hope.

"I have no reason to do so," he answered.

"It exists," she replied. "I know what I am saying; will you not believe me?" As she spoke she glanced hurriedly behind her—footsteps were heard rapidly approaching.

"There is my cousin," she said; "he follows me like a shadow. Dr. Laurier and Mr. Bell, I must see you both, or one of you, in private. I have something of great importance which you ought to know."

Before either of us could answer her, Jasper Bagwell came up. He gave us a polite welcome, and glanced keenly at his cousin, who took no notice of him, but continued her walk.

"Poor girl!" he said with a deep sigh, as we three walked slowly to the house.

"Why do you pity her?" I could not help asking.

"Because she is nearly as much under a delusion as my uncle himself. The fact is she is in the utmost danger, and yet refuses absolutely to believe it. The more eccentric my unfortunate uncle grows, the more she clings to him; she scarcely leaves his side, although it is most unsafe for her to be with him. I think it my absolute duty to watch her day and night, and am really almost worn out with anxiety. The whole of last night I spent in the corridor which divides her room from Mr. Thesiger's. Three times in the course of the night I saw the unfortunate madman gliding down this corridor, and but for my timely appearance on the scene I have not the slightest doubt that he would have entered Helen's room with the most fell design. I see the madness in his eye when he even glances at her. He told me solemnly not later than yesterday that Siva had laid it upon him to take her life, as she was opposed heart and soul to the doctrines of Brahminism, and was a serious obstacle in the way of the great work which my uncle was meant by the idol to undertake. I told Helen exactly what he said, but she goes on as if nothing were wrong. The fact is this, Laurier, if you don't sign that certificate I must get another doctor who will."

Bagwell's communications were certainly alarming, but we had scarcely time to reply to them before we reached the house. When we entered the hall the frown departed from his face like magic, he assumed a thoroughly pleasant manner, and conducted us quickly into the presence of the owner of the house.

Edward Thesiger was a handsome old man, tall and dignified in appearance. He possessed a particularly lofty and intelligent cast of face, aquiline features, and silver hair which flowed down over his shoulders. His face was clean shaven, which allowed the handsome curves of his mobile mouth to be plainly seen. His conversation betokened the man of learning, his words were well chosen, his manner was extremely calm and quiet. At a first glance no one could look more thoroughly sane.

During dinner that night I happened to be seated opposite Miss Thesiger. She was very silent, and seemed terribly depressed. I noticed that she often glanced at her uncle, and further observed that he carefully avoided meeting her eyes. When she came into the room he manifested distinct uneasiness, and when she retired to the drawing-room after dinner a look of relief filled his fine face. He drew up his chair near mine and began to talk.

"I am glad you were able to come," he said. "It is not often one has the privilege of meeting a thoroughly kindred spirit. Now, tell me, have you carefully studied Brahminism?"

"I have done so cursorily," I replied, "and have had from time to time curious dealings with the supernatural." I then added abruptly, "I am much interested to hear from Laurier that you, Mr. Thesiger, possess the idol Siva in this house."

"Hush!" he said, starting and turning very pale. "Do not say the name in such a loud and reckless tone." As he spoke he bent towards me, and his voice dropped. "Mr. Bell, I have extraordinary confidences which I can make to you by-and-by."

"I shall be happy to hear them," I answered.

"Have you had wine enough? Shall we go into the gallery now?"

I rose immediately. My host led me into a conservatory, and from there straight into a marble gallery. It was a curious looking place, being a large oval chamber forty feet long, the walls were faced with marble, and a dado painted in Egyptian style ran round the room. Half way between the middle of the room and the end stood a fountain of curious design. It consisted of the bronze figure of a swan with wings outspread. From its bill the water issued and fell into a circular basin. Facing this fountain, twenty feet away, stood the idol, with its little altar in front of it. I went up and examined it with intense interest. The pedestal on which it rested was about three feet high—the idol itself was the same height, so that its five heads were almost on a level with my face. Round the neck, and decorating each of the heads, were jewels of extraordinary magnificence; the hand which held the trident was loaded with diamond rings. It is almost impossible to describe the sinister effect of this grotesque and horrible monster; and when I saw Mr. Thesiger gazing at it with a peculiar expression of reverence not unmixed with fear, I felt certain that Bagwell was right, and that the man was dangerously insane.

As I was thinking these thoughts my host groaned quite audibly, and then looked steadily at me.

"I am living through a very terrible time," he said in a low voice. "I am the victim of a strange and awful power." Here his words dropped to an intense whisper. "Years ago, when I became a Brahmin," he continued, "voluntarily giving up the faith in which I was born, I little knew to what such a step would lead. I stole Siva from the house of my Indian friend and brought the idol home. From the first it began to exercise a marvellous power over me. I had made a large fortune in India; and when I came to England, bought this place, and finding this curious gallery already in existence, had it lined with marble, and set up Siva in its midst. The study of the faith which I had adopted, the holding of spiritualistic séances and matters of that sort, occupied my time, and I became more and more imbued with the strange mysticism of my belief. As the years flew by I was more and more firmly convinced that what looks like mere wood is in reality imbued with strange and awful qualities. I shall never forget that terrible evening when Siva first spoke to me."

"How long ago was that?" I interrupted.

"Some months ago now. I was kneeling by the altar, and was speaking to him as usual, when I heard words uttered in Hindustanee. At first I could scarcely credit my own ears, but soon I grew accustomed to the fact that Siva wished to hold communication with me, and listened to him nightly. At the beginning of our remarkable intercourse he laid certain mandates upon me which resulted, as you see, in my decorating him with these precious stones. I felt bound to obey him, whatever he dictated; but of late he has told me—he has told me——" The old man began to shudder and tremble.

While he had been speaking to me he had been gazing at the idol; now he walked a few steps away and turned his back on it.

"Sooner or later I must obey him," he said in a feeble voice; "but the thing is driving me crazed—crazed."

"What is it?" I asked; "tell me, I beseech you."

"I cannot; it is too awful—it relates to the one I love best in the world. The sacrifice is too horrible, and yet I am drawn to it—I am drawn to the performing of an awful deed by a terrific power. Ask me no more, Mr. Bell; I see by your face that I have your pity."

"You have, truly," I answered.

I had scarcely said the last words before the door of the gallery was opened, and Miss Thesiger, Bagwell, and Laurier appeared. Miss Thesiger went straight to her uncle's side, and laid her hand on his shoulder.

"Must you stay up any longer?" she asked in a gentle voice. "I heard you walking about last night; you were restless and did not sleep. Do go to bed now; you seem so tired. I know these gentlemen will excuse you," she added, glancing from Laurier to me.

"Certainly," said Laurier. "I should recommend Mr. Thesiger to retire at once; he looks quite worn out."

"I shall go presently—presently," said Thesiger, in a somewhat curt voice. "Leave us, Helen; there's a good child; go, my dear."

"Go, Helen; don't irritate him," I heard Bagwell say.

She gave a quick, despairing glance from one man to the other; then, turning, left the room.

"And now, Mr. Thesiger," I said, "will you not grant me the favour of a séance?"

Mr. Thesiger remained gravely silent for a moment; then he said:

"By virtue of your power as a medium, you may be able to hear the voice, and so convince Dr. Laurier of its reality."

He then proceeded to go through some elaborate operations, and finally kneeling at the altar, began to speak Hindustanee.

It was about the strangest scene I had ever witnessed; and though I stood almost at his elbow, I could hear no sound whatever but his own voice.

"Siva will not speak to-night," he said, rising; "there must be some one here whose influence is adverse. I cannot hear him. It is strange!"

He looked puzzled, and more relieved than otherwise.

"You will go to bed now, sir," said Bagwell; "you look very tired."

"I am," he replied. "I will leave my friends with you, Jasper. You will see that they have all they want." He bade Laurier and me a courteous good-night, nodded to his nephew, and left the room.

"This is the most extraordinary phase of mental delusion I ever heard of," I said. "If you will permit me, Mr. Bagwell, I will examine this idol more particularly."

"You can do so if you please," he said, but he did not speak in a cordial tone.

"Examine it to your heart's content," he continued a moment later; "only pray don't disarrange it—he seems to know by instinct if it is touched. Bah! it is sickening. Shall we go into another room, gentlemen?"

Watching his face carefully, I resolved to make my examination in private, and now followed him into the smoking-room. We stayed there for a short time, talking in a desultory manner, and soon afterwards retired for the night.

On my dressing-table a note awaited me. I opened it hastily, and saw to my surprise that it was from Miss Thesiger.

"I could not get the opportunity I needed to-night," she wrote, "but will you meet me in the Laurel Walk to-morrow morning at five o'clock?"

I tore up the letter after reading it, and soon afterwards got into bed. I must confess that I slept badly that night; I felt worried and anxious. There was not the least doubt that Thesiger was mad; it was all too apparent that his madness was daily and hourly assuming a more and more dangerous form. The affectionate girl who clung to him ought undoubtedly to be removed from his neighbourhood.

At the hour named by Miss Thesiger, I rose, dressed, and stole downstairs through the silent house. I found her as she had indicated in the Laurel Walk.

"How good of you to come!" she said. "But we must not talk here; it would not be safe."

"What do you mean?" I answered. "No one can possibly watch us at this hour."

"Jasper may be about," she said; "as far as I can tell he seems never to sleep. I believe he paces outside my room the greater part of the night."

"You can scarcely blame him for that," I said; "he does it in order to ensure your safety."

She gave me an impatient glance.

"I see he has been talking to you," she replied; "but now it is necessary for you to hear my side of the story. Come into this summer-house; he will never guess that we are here."

Turning abruptly, she led the way into a small, tastefully arranged summer-house. Shutting the door behind her, she turned at once and faced me.

"Now," she said in an eager voice, "I will tell you everything. There is an unexplained mystery about all this, and I am convinced that Jasper is at the bottom of it."

"What do you mean?" I asked.

"I have nothing whatever but a woman's intuition to guide me, but, all the same, I am convinced of what I am saying. Before Jasper came home Uncle Edward was a Brahmin beyond doubt. His séances were intensely disagreeable to me, and I took care never to witness them nor to speak to him on the terrible subject of Siva; but, beyond the fact that he was a Brahmin deeply imbued with the mysteries of his so-called religion, he was a perfectly sane, happy, intelligent, and affectionate man. He loved me devotedly, as I am the child of his favourite brother, and told me just before Jasper's arrival that he had made me his heiress, leaving me all that he possessed in the world. He had never liked Jasper, and was annoyed when he came here and made this house his head-quarters. I had not met my cousin since I was a little child, and when he arrived on the scene took a great dislike to him. He began at once to pay me hateful attentions, and to question me eagerly with regard to Uncle Edward and his ways. By a curious coincidence, he had known this house before he went to India, having stayed here as a boy. He showed particular interest in the oval gallery, and encouraged Uncle Edward to talk of Siva, although he saw that the subject excited him considerably.

"Jasper had been about a fortnight in the house when my poor uncle made, as he considered, the astounding discovery that Siva could speak to him. I shall never forget the first day when he told me of this, the sparkle in his eyes, the tremble of his hands, the nervous energy which seemed to animate him. From that hour day by day came the gradual diminution of strength both of mind and body, the loss of appetite, the feverish touch. All these things puzzled and distressed me, but I could not bear to confide my fears to Jasper.

"These things went on for over a month, and Uncle Edward certainly deteriorated in every way. He spent the greater part of both day and night in the gallery, begging of me to come with him, imploring me to listen for the voice. During that month he spent a large fortune in precious stones for Siva, showing them to me first before he decorated the hideous thing with them. I felt wild with misery, and all the time Jasper was here watching and watching. At the end of the first month there came a distinct change. Uncle Edward, who had been devoted to me up to then, began to show a new attitude. He now began to dislike to have me in his presence, often asking me as a special favour to leave the room. One day he said to me:

"'Do you keep your door locked at night?'

"I laughed when he spoke.

"'Certainly not,' I answered.

"'I wish you would do so,' he said very earnestly; 'will you, as a personal favour to me?'

"Jasper was in the room when he spoke. I saw a queer light flashing through his eyes, and then he bent over his book as if he had not heard.

"'As a special favour to me, keep your door locked, Helen,' said Uncle Edward.

"I made him a soothing answer, and pretended to assent. Of course I never locked my door. Then Jasper began to talk to me. He said that Uncle Edward was not only mad, but that his mania was assuming a terrible form, and against me. He said that my life was in danger—he thought to frighten me— little he knew!"

Here the brave girl drew herself up, indignation sweeping over her face and filling her eyes.

"I told him I did not believe a word of what he said; I declared that Uncle Edward could not hate me—is he not the one I love best in the world? Jasper grew very angry.

"'Look here, Helen,' he said, 'I know enough to lock him up.'

"'To lock him up in a lunatic asylum?' I cried.

"'Yes,' he answered. 'I have only to get two doctors to certify to the fact of his insanity, and the deed is done. I have made up my mind to do it.'

"'You could never be so cruel,' I replied. 'Think of his grey hairs, Jasper,' I pleaded. 'He is the dearest to me in all the world; you could not take his liberty away. Do just respect his one little craze; believe me, he is not really mad. Go away if you are afraid of him; I am not. Oh, why don't you leave us both in peace?'

"'I dare not,' he answered. 'I love you, and I am determined you shall marry me. Engage yourself to me at once, and I will do nothing to take away Uncle Edward's liberty for at least a month.'

"I struggled against this horrible wish of my cousin's, but in the end I yielded to it. I became engaged to him secretly, for he did not wish Uncle Edward to know. I knew, of course, why he wished to marry me; he had heard that I am some day to inherit my uncle's wealth. Jasper himself is a very poor man. Now, Mr. Bell, you know everything. Things get worse and worse, and at times I am almost inclined to believe that my life is in some danger. A fiend has taken possession of the uncle whose heart was so warm and loving. Ah, it is fearful! I do not believe a bitterer trial could be given to any girl—it is too awful to feel that the one she loves best in all the world has changed in his feelings towards her. It is not so much the sacrifice of my poor life I mind as the feeling that things are so bitterly altered with him. Jasper put an alternative to me last night. Either I am to marry him within a week, or I am to use my influence to induce Dr. Laurier to sign the certificate. If I accept neither proposal, he will get down two other doctors from London for the purpose."

"What have you decided to do?" I asked.

"I will marry Jasper; yes, within a week I shall be his wife, unless something happens to show us what is the meaning of this fearful mystery, for I cannot—never, never can I deprive Uncle Edward of his liberty."

"I am glad you have confided in me," I said after a pause, "and I will do my utmost for you. When did you say that your uncle first heard the idol speak?"

"Two or three months ago now, soon after Jasper came home. Mr. Bell, is there any chance of your being able to help me?"

"I will promise to do my utmost, but just at present I can see no special light. By the way, would it not be well for you to leave The Hynde for a short time?"

"No, I am not at all afraid; I can take care of myself. It is not my dear uncle whom I fear; it is Jasper."

Soon afterwards she left me, and as it was still quite early, and the servants were not yet even up, I considered that an excellent opportunity had occurred for examining the idol.

I made my way to the gallery, and softly opening the door, stole in. The bright sunlight which was now flooding the chamber seemed to rob the grotesque old idol of half its terrors, and I made up my mind not to leave a stone unturned to discover if any foul play in connection with it could possibly be perpetrated. But the impossibility of such being the case seemed more and more evident as I went on with my search. Only a pigmy could be secreted inside the idol. There was no vulgar form of deception possible on the lines, for instance, of the ancient priests of Pompeii who conducted a speaking-tube to an idol's mouth. Siva was not even standing by the wall, thus precluding the possibility of the sounds being conducted on the plan of a whispering gallery. No—I was, against my own will, forced to the absolute conviction that the voice was an hallucination of the diseased mind of Edward Thesiger.

I was just going to abandon my investigations and return to my own room, when, more by chance than design, I knelt down for a moment at the little altar. As I was about to rise I noticed something rather odd. I listened attentively. It was certainly remarkable. As I knelt I could just hear a low, continuous hissing sound. Directly I moved away it ceased. As I tried it several times with the same invariable result, I became seriously puzzled to account for it. What devilry could be at work to produce this? Was it possible that some one was playing a trick on *me*?—and if so, by what means?

I glanced rapidly round, and as I did so a mad thought struck me. I hurried across to the fountain and put my ear close to the swan's mouth, from which a tiny jet of water was issuing. The low, scarcely audible noise that the water made as it flowed out through the swan's bill was exactly the same sound I had heard nearly twenty feet away at the altar. The enormity of the situation stunned me for a moment, then gradually, piece by piece, the plot revealed itself.

The shape of the gallery was a true oval, a geometrical ellipse, the extraordinary acoustic properties of which I knew well. This peculiarly shaped gallery contained two foci—one towards each end—and the nature of the curve of the walls was such that sound issuing from either focus was directed by reflection at various points to the other focus, and to the other focus alone. Even across an enormous distance between such would be the case. The swan's mouth was evidently at one focus; the position of a man's head as he knelt at the altar would be without the slightest doubt at the other. Could the pipe be used as a speaking-tube when the water was turned off?

I felt so excited by this extraordinary discovery that it was only with an effort that I maintained my self-control. I knew that presence of mind was absolutely necessary in order to expose this horrible scheme. I left the gallery and passed through the conservatory. Here I found the gardener arranging some pots. I chatted to him for a few moments. He looked surprised at seeing me up at such an unusual hour.

"Can you tell me how the fountain in the gallery is turned on or off?" I asked.

"Yes, I can, sir," he replied; "the pipe runs along outside this stand, and here's the tap."

I went across and looked at it. In the leaden pipe that was fastened to the wall were two nuts, which could be turned by a small spanner, and between them was a brass cap, which fitted on to a circular outlet from the pipe.

"What is this used for?" I asked, pointing to the little outlet which was closed by the cap.

"We screw the hose on there, sir, to water the flowers."

"I see," I answered; "so when you use the hose you shut off the water from the fountain in the gallery."

"That's it, sir, and a wonderful deal of trouble it saves. Why it was never done before I can't think."

"When was it done, then?" I asked. My heart was beating fast.

"It was Mr. Bagwell's thought, sir; he had it fixed on soon after he came. He wanted to have plenty of water handy in order to water the plants he brought back from India; but, lor! sir, they'll never live through the winter, even under glass."

I waited to hear no more—the whole infernal plot was laid bare. The second tap, which shut off the water both from the fountain and the hose pipe, was, of course, quite useless, except for Bagwell's evil purpose.

I hurried straight up to Laurier's room. He was just preparing to rise. His astonishment when I told him of my discovery was beyond words.

"Then, by shutting off the water, and applying his mouth to the place where the hose is fixed on, he could convey his voice to the swan's mouth like an ordinary speaking-tube, which, owing to the peculiar construction of the gallery, would be carried across to the other focus at the altar?" he said.

"Exactly," I replied. "And now, Dr. Laurier, you must please allow me to regulate our future plans. They're simply these. You must tell Bagwell that you absolutely refuse to sign the certificate unless Thesiger declares that he hears the voice again in your presence, and arrange that the séance takes place at nine o'clock to-night. I in the meantime shall ostensibly take my departure, and so leave the ground clear for Bagwell. He is evidently rather afraid of me. My going will throw him completely off his guard; but I shall in reality only leave the train at the next station and return here after dark. You will have to see that the conservatory door leading on to the terrace is left unlocked. I shall steal in, and, hiding myself in the conservatory, shall await Bagwell. You in the meantime will be in the gallery with Thesiger. When you hear me call out, come in at once. Our only hope is to take that wretch red-handed."

To this hastily constructed scheme Laurier instantly agreed, and at four o'clock that afternoon I took my leave, Miss Thesiger, looking white and miserable, standing on the steps to see me off. Bagwell drove me himself to the station, and bade me good-bye with a heartiness which was at least sincere.

I was back again at The Hynde at half-past eight that evening. Laurier had left the conservatory door unlocked, and, slipping in, it being now quite dark, I hid myself behind some large flowering shrubs and waited. Presently I heard the door of the conservatory open, and in stole Bagwell. I saw him approach the pipe, turn the spanner which shut off the water from the fountain and also from the hose pipe, and then proceed to unscrew the brass cap. I waited till I saw him place his mouth to the opening and begin to speak, and then I dashed out upon him and called loudly for Laurier. Bagwell's surprise and terror at my unexpected attack absolutely bereft him of speech, and he stood gazing at me with a mixed expression of fury and fear. The next minute Laurier and Thesiger both burst in from the gallery. I still retained my hold of Bagwell. The moment I saw the sign, I went up to him, and in a few words explained the whole fraud. But it was not until I had demonstrated the trick in the oval gallery that he became convinced; then the relief on his face was marvellous.

"You leave my house at once," he said to Bagwell; "go, sir, if you do not wish to be in the hands of the police. Where is Helen? where is my child?"

He had scarcely said the words, and Bagwell was just slinking off with a white face like a whipped cur towards the door, when Helen appeared upon the scene.

"What is it?" she cried. "Is anything the matter?"

The old man strode up to her; he took her in his arms.

"It is all right, Helen," he said, "all right. I can never explain; but, take my word, it is all right. I was a fool, and worse—nay, I was mad—but I am sane now. Mr. Bell, I can never express my obligations to you. But now, will you do one thing more?"

"What is that? Be assured I will do anything in my power," I answered.

"Then return here to-night and destroy Siva. How I could have been infatuated enough to believe in that senseless piece of wood is beyond my power to understand. But destroy it, sir; take it away; let me never lay eyes on it again."

Early on the following morning, when I was leaving the house, Bagwell, who must have been waiting for the purpose, suddenly stepped across my path.

"I have a word of explanation to give," he said. "You, Mr. Bell, have won, and I have lost. I played a deep game and for a large cause. It did not occur to me as possible that any one could discover the means by which I made Siva speak. I am now about to leave England for ever, but before I do so, it may interest you to know that the temptation offered to me was a very peculiar and strong one. I had not been an hour at the Hynde before I suddenly remembered having spent some months in the old house when a boy. I recollected the oval gallery. Its peculiar acoustic qualities had been pointed out to me by a scientist who happened to live there at the time. The desire to win, not Helen, but my uncle's property, was too strong to be resisted by a penniless man. My object was to terrify Thesiger, whose brain was already nearly overbalanced, into complete insanity, get him locked up, and marry Helen. How I succeeded, and in the end failed, you know well!"

TO PROVE AN ALIBI

I first met Arthur Cressley in the late spring of 1892. I had been spending the winter in Egypt, and was returning to Liverpool. One calm evening, about eleven o'clock, while we were still in the Mediterranean, I went on deck to smoke a final cigar before turning in. After pacing up and down for a time I leant over the taff-rail and began idly watching the tiny wavelets with their crests of white fire as they rippled away from the vessel's side. Presently I became aware of some one standing near me, and, turning, saw that it was one of my fellow-passengers, a young man whose name I knew but whose acquaintance I had not yet made. He was entered in the passenger list as Arthur Cressley, belonged to an old family in Derbyshire, and was returning home from Western Australia, where he had made a lot of money. I offered him a light, and after a few preliminary remarks we drifted into a desultory conversation. He told me that he had been in Australia for fifteen years, and having done well was now returning to settle in his native land.

"Then you do not intend going out again?" I asked.

"No," he replied; "I would not go through the last fifteen years for double the money I have made."

"I suppose you will make London your headquarters?"

"Not altogether; but I shall have to spend a good deal of time there. My wish is for a quiet country life, and I intend to take over the old family property. We have a place called Cressley Hall, in Derbyshire, which has belonged to us for centuries. It would be a sort of white elephant, for it has fallen into pitiable decay; but, luckily, I am now in a position to restore it and set it going again in renewed prosperity."

"You are a fortunate man," I answered.

"Perhaps I am," he replied. "Yes, as far as this world's goods go I suppose I am lucky, considering that I arrived in

Australia fifteen years ago with practically no money in my pocket. I shall be glad to be home again for many reasons, chiefly because I can save the old property from being sold."

"It is always a pity when a fine old family seat has to go to the hammer for want of funds," I remarked.

"That is true, and Cressley Hall is a superb old place. There is only one drawback to it; but I don't believe there is anything in that," added Cressley in a musing tone.

Knowing him so little I did not feel justified in asking for an explanation. I waited, therefore, without speaking. He soon proceeded:

"I suppose I am rather foolish about it," he continued; "but if I am superstitious, I have abundant reason. For more than a century and a half there has been a strange fatality about any Cressley occupying the Hall. This fatality was first exhibited in 1700, when Barrington Cressley, one of the most aban-doned libertines of that time, led his infamous orgies there— of these even history takes note. There are endless legends as to their nature, one of which is that he had personal dealings with the devil in the large turret room, the principal bedroom at the Hall, and was found dead there on the following morn-ing. Certainly since that date a curious doom has hung over the family, and this doom shows itself in a strange way, only attacking those victims who are so unfortunate as to sleep in the turret room. Gilbert Cressley, the young Court favourite of George the Third, was found mysteriously murdered there, and my own great-grandfather paid the penalty by losing his reason within those gloomy walls."

"If the room has such an evil reputation, I wonder that it is occupied," I replied.

"It happens to be far and away the best bedroom in the house, and people always laugh at that sort of thing until they are brought face to face with it. The owner of the property is not only born there, as a rule, but also breathes his last in the old four-poster, the most extraordinary, wonderful old bed-stead you ever laid eyes on. Of course I do not believe in any malevolent influences from the unseen world, but the record of disastrous coincidences in that one room is, to say the least of it, curious. Not that this sort of thing will deter me from going into possession, and I intend to put a lot of money into Cressley Hall."

"Has no one been occupying it lately?" I asked.

"Not recently. An old housekeeper has had charge of the place for the last few years. The agent had orders to sell the Hall long ago, but though it has been in the market for a long time I do not believe there was a single offer. Just before I left Australia I wired to Murdock, my agent, that I intended taking over the place, and authorised its withdrawal from the market."

"Have you no relations?" I inquired.

"None at all. Since I have been away my only brother died. It is curious to call it going home when one has no relatives and only friends who have probably forgotten one."

I could not help feeling sorry for Cressley as he described the lonely outlook. Of course, with heaps of money and an old family place he would soon make new friends; but he looked the sort of chap who might be imposed upon, and although he was as nice a fellow as I had ever met, I could not help coming to the conclusion that he was not specially strong, either mentally or physically. He was essentially good-looking, however, and had the indescribable bearing of a man of old family. I wondered how he had managed to make his money. What he told me about his old Hall also excited my interest, and as we talked I managed to allude to my own peculiar hobby, and the delight I took in such old legends.

As the voyage flew by our acquaintance grew apace, ripening into a warm friendship. Cressley told me much of his past life, and finally confided to me one of his real objects in returning to England.

While prospecting up country he had come across some rich veins of gold, and now his intention was to bring out a large syndicate in order to acquire the whole property, which, he anticipated, was worth at least a million. He spoke confidently of this great scheme, but always wound up by informing me that the money which he hoped to make was only of interest to him for the purpose of re-establishing Cressley Hall in its ancient splendour.

As we talked I noticed once or twice that a man stood near us who seemed to take an interest in our conversation. He was a thickly set individual with a florid complexion and a broad German cast of face. He was an inveterate smoker, and when he stood near us with a pipe in his mouth the expression of his face was almost a blank; but watching him closely I saw a look in his eyes which betokened the shrewd man of business, and I could scarcely tell why, but I felt uncomfortable in his presence. This man, Wickham by name, managed to pick up an acquaintance with Cressley, and soon they spent a good deal of time together. They made a contrast as they paced up and down on deck, or played cards in the evening; the Englishman being slight and almost fragile in build, the German of the bulldog order, with a manner at once curt and overbearing. I took a dislike to Wickham, and wondered what Cressley could see in him.

"Who is the fellow?" I asked on one occasion, linking my hand in Cressley's arm and drawing him aside as I spoke.

"Do you mean Wickham?" he answered. "I am sure I cannot tell you. I never met the chap before this voyage. He came on board at King George's Sound, where I also embarked; but he never spoke to me until we were in the Mediterranean. On the whole, Bell, I am inclined to like him; he seems to be downright and honest. He knows a great deal about the bush, too, as he has spent several years there."

"And he gives you the benefit of his information?" I asked.

"I don't suppose he knows more than I do, and it is doubtful whether he has had so rough a time."

"Then in that case he picks your brains."

"What do you mean?"

The young fellow looked at me with those clear grey eyes which were his most attractive feature.

"Nothing," I answered, "nothing; only if you will be guided by a man nearly double your age, I would take care to tell Wickham as little as possible. Have you ever observed that he happens to be about when you and I are engaged in serious conversation?"

"I can't say that I have."

"Well, keep your eyes open and you'll see what I mean. Be as friendly as you like, but don't give him your confidence—that is all."

"You are rather late in advising me on that score," said Cressley, with a somewhat nervous laugh. "Wickham knows all about the old Hall by this time."

"And your superstitious fears with regard to the turret room?" I queried.

"Well, I have hinted at them. You will be surprised, but he is full of sympathy."

"Tell him no more," I said in conclusion.

Cressley made a sort of half-promise, but looked as if he rather resented my interference.

A day or two later we reached Liverpool; I was engaged long ago to stay with some friends in the suburbs, and Cressley took up his abode at the Prince's Hotel. His property was some sixty miles away, and when we parted he insisted on my agreeing to come down and see his place as soon as he had put things a little straight.

I readily promised to do so, provided we could arrange a visit before my return to London.

Nearly a week went by and I saw nothing of Cressley; then, on a certain morning, he called to see me.

"How are you getting on?" I asked.

"Capitally," he replied. "I have been down to the Hall several times with my agent, Murdock, and though the place is in the most shocking condition I shall soon put things in order. But what I have come specially to ask you now is whether you can get away to-day and come with me to the Hall for a couple of nights. I had arranged with the agent to go down this afternoon in his company, but he has been suddenly taken ill—he is rather bad, I believe—and cannot possibly come with me. He has ordered the housekeeper to get a couple of rooms ready, and though I am afraid it will be rather roughing it, I shall be awfully glad if you can come."

I had arranged to meet a man in London on special business that very evening, and could not put him off; but my irresistible desire to see the old place from the description I had heard of it decided me to make an effort to fall in as well as I could with Cressley's plans.

"I wish I could go with you to-day," I said; "but that, as it happens, is out of the question. I must run up to town on some pressing business; but if you will allow me I can easily come back again to-morrow. Can you not put off your visit until to-morrow evening?"

"No, I am afraid I cannot do that. I have to meet several of the tenants, and have made all arrangements to go by the five o'clock train this afternoon."

He looked depressed at my refusal, and after a moment said thoughtfully:

"I wish you could have come with me to-day. When Murdock could not come I thought of you at once—it would have made all the difference."

"I am sorry," I replied; "but I can promise faithfully to be with you to-morrow. I shall enjoy seeing your wonderful old Hall beyond anything; and as to roughing it, I am used to that. You will not mind spending one night there by yourself?"

He looked at me as if he were about to speak, but no words came from his lips.

"What is the matter?" I said, giving him an earnest glance. "By the way, are you going to sleep in the turret room?"

"I am afraid there is no help for it; the housekeeper is certain to get it ready for me. The owner of the property always sleeps there, and it would look like a confession of weakness to ask to be put into another bedroom."

"Nevertheless, if you are nervous, I should not mind that," I said.

"Oh, I don't know that I am absolutely nervous, Bell, but all the same I have a superstition. At the present moment I have the queerest sensation; I feel as if I ought not to pay this visit to the Hall."

"If you intend to live there by-and-by, you must get over this sort of thing," I remarked.

"Oh yes, I must, and I would not yield to it on any account whatever. I am sorry I even mentioned it to you. It is good of you to promise to come to-morrow, and I shall look forward to seeing you. By what train will you come?"

We looked up the local time-table, and I decided on a train which would leave Liverpool about five o'clock.

"The very one that I shall go down by to-day," said Cressley; "that's capital, I'll meet you with a conveyance of some sort and drive you over. The house is a good two hours' drive from the station, and you cannot get a trap there for love or money."

"By the way," I said, "is there much the matter with your agent?"

"I cannot tell you; he seems bad enough. I went up to his house this morning and saw the wife. It appears that he was suddenly taken ill with a sort of asthmatic attack to which he is subject. While I was talking to Mrs. Murdock, a messenger came down to say that her husband specially wished to see me, so we both went to his room, but he had dozed off into a queer restless sleep before we arrived. The wife said he must not be awakened on any account, but I caught a glimpse of him and he certainly looked bad, and was moaning as if in a good deal of pain. She gave me the keys of a bureau in his room, and I took out some estimates, and left a note for him telling him to come on as soon as he was well enough."

"And your visit to his room never roused him?" I said.

"No, although Mrs. Murdock and I made a pretty good bit of noise moving about and opening and shutting drawers. His moans were quite heartrending—he was evidently in considerable pain; and I was glad to get away, as that sort of thing always upsets me."

"Who is this Murdock?" I asked.

"Oh, the man who has looked after the place for years. I was referred to him by my solicitors. He seems a most capable person, and I hope to goodness he won't be ill long. If he is I shall find myself in rather a fix."

I made no reply to this, and soon afterwards Cressley shook hands with me and departed on his way. I went to my room, packed my belongings, and took the next train to town. The business which I had to get through occupied the whole of that evening and also some hours of the following day. I found I was not able to start for Liverpool before the 12.10 train at Euston, and should not therefore arrive at Lime Street before five o'clock—too late to catch the train for Brent, the nearest station to Cressley's place. Another train left Central Station for Brent, however, at seven o'clock, and I determined to wire to Cressley to tell him to meet me by the latter train. This was the last train in the day, but there was no fear of my missing it.

I arrived at Lime Street almost to the moment and drove straight to the Prince's Hotel, where I had left my bag the day before. Here a telegram awaited me; it was from Cressley, and ran as follows:—

> "Hope this will reach you time; if so, call at Murdock's house, No. 12, Melville Gardens. If possible see him and get the documents referred to in Schedule A—he will know what you mean. Most important.
> "Cressley"

I glanced at the clock in the hall; it was now a quarter past five—my train would leave at seven. I had plenty of time to get something to eat and then go to Murdock's.

Having despatched my telegram to Cressley, telling him to look out for me by the train which arrived at Brent at nine o'clock, I ordered a meal, ate it, and then hailing a cab, gave the driver the number of Murdock's house. Melville Gardens was situated somewhat in the suburbs, and it was twenty minutes' drive from my hotel. When we drew up at Murdock's door I told the cabman to wait, and, getting out, rang the bell. The servant who answered my summons told me that the agent was still very ill and could not be seen by any one. I then inquired for the wife. I was informed that she was out, but would be back soon. I looked at my watch. It was just six o'clock. I determined to wait to see Mrs. Murdock if possible.

Having paid and dismissed my cab, I was shown into a small, untidily kept parlour, where I was left to my own meditations. The weather was hot and the room close. I paced up and down restlessly. The minutes flew by and Mrs. Murdock did not put in an appearance. I looked at my watch, which now pointed to twenty minutes past six. It would take me, in an ordinary cab, nearly twenty minutes to reach the station. In order to make all safe I ought to leave Murdock's house in ten minutes from now at the latest.

I went and stood by the window watching anxiously for Mrs. Murdock to put in an appearance. Melville Gardens was a somewhat lonely place, and few people passed the house, which was old and shabby; it had evidently not been done up for years. I was just turning round in order to ring the bell to leave a message with the servant, when the room door was opened and, to my astonishment, in walked Wickham, the man I had last seen on board the *Euphrates*. He came up to me at once and held out his hand.

"No doubt you are surprised at seeing me here, Mr. Bell," he exclaimed.

"I certainly was for a moment," I answered; but then I added, "The world is a small place, and one soon gets accustomed to acquaintances cropping up in all sorts of unlikely quarters."

"Why unlikely?" said Wickham. "Why should I not know Murdock, who happens to be a very special and very old friend of mine? I might as well ask you why you are interested in him."

"Because I happen to be a friend of Arthur Cressley's," I answered, "and have come here on his business."

"And so am I also a friend of Cressley's. He has asked me to go and see him at Cressley Hall some day, and I hope to avail myself of his invitation. The servant told me that you were waiting for Mrs Murdock—can I give her any message from you?"

"I want to see Murdock himself," I said, after a pause. "Do you think that it is possible for me to have an interview with him?"

"I left him just now and he was asleep," said Wickham. "He is still very ill, and I think the doctor is a little anxious about him. It would not do to disturb him on any account. Of course, if he happens to awake he might be able to tell you what you want to know. By the way, has it anything to do with Cressley Hall?"

"Yes; I have just had a telegram from Cressley, and the message is somewhat important. You are quite sure that Murdock is asleep?"

"He was when I left the room, but I will go up again and see. Are you going to London to-night, Mr. Bell?"

"No; I am going down to Cressley Hall, and must catch the seven o'clock train. I have not a moment to wait." As I spoke I took out my watch.

"It only wants five-and-twenty minutes to seven," I said, "and I never care to run a train to the last moment. There is no help for it, I suppose I must go without seeing Murdock. Cressley will in all probability send down a message to-morrow for the papers he requires."

"Just stay a moment," said Wickham, putting on an anxious expression; "it is a great pity that you should not see

Cressley's agent if it is as vital as all that. Ah! and here comes Mrs. Murdock; wait one moment, I'll go and speak to her."

He went out of the room, and I heard him say something in a low voice in the passage—a woman's voice replied, and the next instant Mrs. Murdock stood before me. She was a tall woman with a sallow face and sandy hair; she had a blank sort of stare about her, and scarcely any expression. Now she fixed her dull, light-blue eyes on my face and held out her hand.

"You are Mr. Bell?" she said. "I have heard of you, of course, from Mr. Cressley. So you are going to spend to-night with him at Cressley Hall. I am glad, for it is a lonely place—the most lonely place I know."

"Pardon me," I interrupted, "I cannot stay to talk to you now or I shall miss my train. Can I see your husband or can I not?"

She glanced at Wickham, then she said with hesitation,—

"If he is asleep it would not do to disturb him, but there is a chance of his being awake now. I don't quite understand about the papers, I wish I did. It would be best for you to see him certainly; follow me upstairs."

"And I tell you what," called Wickham after us, "I'll go and engage a cab, so that you shall lose as short a time as possible, Mr. Bell."

I thanked him and followed the wife upstairs. The stairs were narrow and steep, and we soon reached the small landing at the top. Four bedrooms opened into it. Mrs. Murdock turned the handle of the one which exactly faced the stairs, and we both entered. Here the blinds were down, and the chamber was considerably darkened. The room was a small one, and the greater part of the space was occupied by an old-fashioned Albert bedstead with the curtains pulled forward. Within I could just see the shadowy outline of a figure, and I distinctly heard the feeble groans of the sick man.

"Ah! what a pity, my husband is still asleep," said Mrs. Murdock, as she turned softly round to me and put her finger to her lips. "It would injure him very much to awaken him," she said. "You can go and look at him if you like; you will see how very ill he is. I wonder if I could help you with regard to the papers you want, Mr. Bell?"

"I want the documents referred to in Schedule A," I answered.

"Schedule A?" she repeated, speaking under her breath. "I remember that name. Surely all the papers relating to it are in this drawer. I think I can get them for you."

She crossed the room as she spoke, and standing with her back to the bedstead, took a bunch of keys from a table which stood near and fitted one into the lock of a high bureau made of mahogany. She pulled open a drawer and began to examine its contents.

While she was so occupied I approached the bed, and bending slightly forward, took a good stare at the sick man. I had never seen Murdock before. There was little doubt that he was ill—he looked very ill, indeed. His face was long and cadaverous, the cheek bones were high, and the cheeks below were much sunken in; the lips, which were clean-shaven, were slightly drawn apart, and some broken irregular teeth were visible. The eyebrows were scanty, and the hair was much worn away from the high and hollow forehead. The man looked sick unto death. I had seldom seen any one with an expression like his—the closed eyes were much sunken, and the moaning which came from the livid lips was horrible to listen to.

After giving Murdock a long and earnest stare, I stepped back from the bed, and was just about to speak to Mrs. Murdock, who was rustling papers in the drawer, when the most strong and irresistible curiosity assailed me. I could not account for it, but I felt bound to yield to its suggestions. I turned again and bent close over the sick man. Surely there was something monotonous about that deep-drawn breath; those moans, too, came at wonderfully regular intervals. Scarcely knowing why I did it, I stretched out my hand and laid it on the forehead. Good God! what was the matter? I felt myself turning cold; the perspiration stood out on my own brow. I had not touched a living forehead at all. Flesh was flesh, it was impossible to mistake the feel, but there was no flesh here. The figure in the bed was neither a living nor a dead man, it was a wax representation of one; but why did it moan, and how was it possible for it not to breathe?

Making the greatest effort of my life, I repressed an exclamation, and when Mrs. Murdock approached me with the necessary papers in her hand, took them from her in my usual manner.

"These all relate to Schedule A," she said. "I hope I am not doing wrong in giving them to you without my husband's leave. He looks very ill, does he not?"

"He looks as bad as he can look," I answered. I moved towards the door. Something in my tone must have alarmed her, for a curious expression of fear dilated the pupils of her light blue eyes. She followed me downstairs. A hansom was waiting for me. I nodded to Wickham, did not even wait to shake hands with Mrs. Murdock, and sprang into the cab.

"Central Station!" I shouted to the man; and then as he whipped up his horse and flew down the street, "A sovereign if you get there before seven o'clock."

We were soon dashing quickly along the streets. I did not know Liverpool well, and consequently could not exactly tell where the man was going. When I got into the hansom it wanted twelve minutes to seven o'clock; these minutes were quickly flying, and still no station.

"Are you sure you are going right?" I shouted through the hole in the roof.

"You'll be there in a minute, sir," he answered. "It's Lime Street Station you want, isn't it?"

"No; Central Station," I answered. "I told you Central Station; drive there at once like the very devil. I must catch that train, for it is the last one to-night."

"All right, sir; I can do it," he cried, whipping up his horse again.

Once more I pulled out my watch; the hands pointed to three minutes to seven.

At ten minutes past we were driving into the station. I flung the man half a sovereign, and darted into the booking-office.

"To Brent, sir? The last train has just gone," said the clerk, with an impassive stare at me through the little window.

I flung my bag down in disgust and swore a great oath. But for that idiot of a driver I should have just caught the train. All of a sudden a horrible thought flashed through my brain. Had the cabman been bribed by Wickham? No directions could have been plainer than mine. I had told the man to drive to Central Station. Central Station did not sound the least like Lime Street Station. How was it possible for him to make so grave a mistake?

The more I considered the matter the more certain I was that a black plot was brewing, and that Wickham was in the thick of it. My brain began to whirl with excitement. What was the matter? Why was a lay figure in Murdock's bed? Why had I been taken upstairs to see it? Without any doubt both Mrs. Murdock and Wickham wished me to see what was such an admirable imitation of a sick man—an imitation so good, with those ghastly moans coming from the lips, that it would have taken in the sharpest detective in Scotland Yard. I myself was deceived until I touched the forehead. This state of things had not been brought to pass without a reason. What was the reason? Could it be possible that Murdock was wanted elsewhere, and it was thought well that I should see him in order to prove an alibi, should he be suspected of a ghastly crime? My God! what could this mean? From the first I had mistrusted Wickham. What was he doing in Murdock's house? For what purpose had he bribed the driver of the cab in order to make me lose my train?

The more I thought, the more certain I was that Cressley was in grave danger; and I now determined, cost what it might, to get to him that night.

I left the station, took a cab, and drove back to my hotel. I asked to see the manager. A tall, dark man in a frock-coat emerged from a door at the back of the office and inquired what he could do for me. I begged permission to speak to him alone, and we passed into his private room.

"I am in an extraordinary position," I began. "Circumstances of a private nature make it absolutely necessary that I should go to a place called Cressley Hall, about fourteen miles from Brent. Brent is sixty miles down the line, and the last train has gone. I could take a 'special,' but there might be an interminable delay at Brent, and I prefer to drive straight to Cressley Hall across country. Can you assist me by directing me to some good job-master from whom I can hire a carriage and horses?"

The man looked at me with raised eyebrows. He evidently thought I was mad.

"I mean what I say," I added, "and am prepared to back my words with a substantial sum. Can you help me?"

"I dare say you might get a carriage and horses to do it," he replied; "but it is a very long way, and over a hilly country. No two horses could go such a distance without rest. You would have to change from time to time as you went. I will send across to the hotel stables for my man, and you can see him about it."

He rang the bell and gave his orders. In a few moments the job-master came in. I hurriedly explained to him what I wanted ed. At first he said it was impossible, that his best horses were out, and that those he had in his stables could not possibly attempt such a journey; but when I brought out my cheque-book and offered to advance any sum in reason, he hesitated.

"Of course there is one way in which it might be managed, sir. I would take you myself as far as Ovenden, which is five-and-twenty miles from here. There, I know, we could get a pair of fresh horses from the Swan; and if we wired at once from here, horses might be ready at Carlton, which is another twenty miles on the road. But, at our best, sir, it will be between two and three in the morning before we get to Brent."

"I am sorry to hear you say so," I answered; "but it is better to arrive then than to wait until to-morrow. Please send the necessary telegram off without a moment's delay, and get the carriage ready."

"Put the horses in at once, John," said the manager. "You had better take the light wagonette. You ought to get there between one and two in the morning with that."

Then he added, as the man left the room,—

"I suppose, sir, your business is very urgent?"

"It is," I replied shortly.

He looked as if he would like to question me further, but refrained.

A few moments later I had taken my seat beside the driver, and we were speeding at a good round pace through the streets of Liverpool. We passed quickly through the suburbs, and out into the open country. The evening was a lovely one, and the country looked its best. It was difficult to believe, as I drove through the peaceful landscape, that in all probability a dark deed was in contemplation, and that the young man to whom I had taken a most sincere liking was in danger of his life.

As I drove silently by my companion's side I reviewed the whole situation. The more I thought of it the less I liked it. On board the *Euphrates* Wickham had been abnormally interested in Cressley. Cressley had himself confided to him his superstitious dread with regard to the turret room. Cressley had come home with a fortune; and if he floated his syndicate he would be a millionaire. Wickham scarcely looked like a rich man. Then why should he know Murdock, and why should a lay figure be put in Murdock's bed? Why, also, through a most unnatural accident, should I have lost my train?

The more I thought, the graver and graver became my fears. Gradually darkness settled over the land, and then a rising moon flooded the country in its weird light. I had been on many a wild expedition before, but in some ways never a wilder than this. Its very uncertainty, wrapped as it was in unformed suspicions, gave it an air of inexpressible mystery.

On and on we went, reaching Ovenden between nine and ten at night. Here horses were ready for us, and we again started on our way. When we got to Carlton, however, there came a hitch in my well-formed arrangements. We drew up at the little inn, to find the place in total darkness, and all the inhabitants evidently in bed and asleep. With some difficulty we roused the landlord, and asked why the horses which had been telegraphed for had not been got ready.

"We did not get them when the second telegram arrived," was the reply.

"The second telegram!" I cried, my heart beating fast. "What do you mean?"

"There were two, sir, both coming from the same stables. The first was written desiring us to have the horses ready at any cost. The second contradicted the first, and said that the gentleman had changed his mind, and was not going. On receipt of that, sir, I shut up the house as usual, and we all went to bed. I am very sorry if there has been any mistake."

"There has, and a terrible one," I could not help muttering under my breath. My fears were getting graver than ever. Who had sent the second telegram? Was it possible that I had been followed by Wickham, who took these means of circumventing me?

"We must get horses, and at once," I said. "Never mind about the second telegram; it was a mistake."

Peach, the jobmaster, muttered an oath.

"I can't understand what is up," he said. He looked mystified and not too well pleased. Then he added,—

"These horses can't go another step, sir."

"They must if we can get no others," I said. I went up to him, and began to whisper in his ear.

"This is a matter of life and death, my good friend. Only the direst necessity takes me on this journey. The second telegram without doubt was sent by a man whom I am trying to circumvent. I know what I am saying. We must get horses, or these must go on. We have not an instant to lose. There is a conspiracy afoot to do serious injury to the owner of Cressley Hall."

"What! the young gentleman who has just come from Australia? You don't mean to say he is in danger?" said Peach.

"He is in the gravest danger. I don't mind who knows. I have reason for my fears."

While I was speaking the landlord drew near. He overheard some of my last words. The landlord and Peach now exchanged glances. After a moment the landlord spoke,—

"A neighbour of ours, sir, has got two good horses," he said. "He is the doctor in this village. I believe he'll lend them if the case is as urgent as you say."

"Go and ask him," I cried. "You shall have ten pounds if we are on the road in five minutes from the present moment."

At this hint the landlord flew. He came back in an incredibly short space of time, accompanied by the doctor's coachman leading the horses. They were quickly harnessed to the wagonette, and once more we started on our way.

"Now drive as you never drove before in the whole course of your life," I said to Peach. "Money is no object. We have still fifteen miles to go, and over a rough country. You can claim any reward in reason if you get to Cressley Hall within an hour."

"It cannot be done, sir," he replied; but then he glanced at me, and some of the determination in my face was reflected in his. He whipped up the horses. They were thoroughbred animals, and worked well under pressure.

We reached the gates of Cressley Hall between two and three in the morning. Here I thought it best to draw up, and told my coachman that I should not need his services any longer.

"If you are afraid of mischief, sir, would it not be best for me to lie about here?" he asked. "I'd rather be in the neighbourhood in case you want me. I am interested in this here job, sir."

"You may well be, my man. God grant it is not a black business. Well, walk the horses up and down, if you like. If you see nothing of me within the next couple of hours, judge that matters are all right, and return with the horses to Carlton."

This being arranged, I turned from Peach and entered the lodge gates. Just inside was a low cottage surrounded by trees. I paused for a moment to consider what I had better do. My difficulty now was how to obtain admittance to the Hall, for of course it would be shut up and all its inhabitants asleep at this hour. Suddenly an idea struck me. I determined to knock up the lodge-keeper, and to enlist her assistance. I went across to the door, and presently succeeded in rousing the inmates. A woman of about fifty appeared. I explained to her my position, and begged of her to give me her help. She hesitated at first in unutterable astonishment; but then, seeing something in my face which convinced her, I suppose, of the truth of my story, for it was necessary to alarm her in order to induce her to do anything, she said she would do what I wished.

"I know the room where Mitchell, the old housekeeper, sleeps," she said, "and we can easily wake him by throwing stones up at his window. If you'll just wait a minute I'll put a shawl over my head and go with you."

She ran into an inner room and quickly re-appeared. Together we made our way along the drive which, far as I could see, ran through a park studded with old timber. We went round the house to the back entrance, and the woman, after a delay of two or three moments, during which I was on thorns, managed to wake up Mitchell the housekeeper. He came to his window, threw it open, and poked out his head.

"What can be wrong?" he said.

"It is Mr. Bell, James," was the reply, "the gentleman who has been expected at the Hall all the evening; he has come now, and wants you to admit him."

The old man said that he would come downstairs. He did so, and opening a door, stood in front of it, barring my entrance.

"Are you really the gentleman Mr. Cressley has been expecting?" he said.

"I am," I replied; "I missed my train, and was obliged to drive out. There is urgent need why I should see your master immediately; where is he?"

"I hope in bed, sir, and asleep; it is nearly three o'clock in the morning."

"Never mind the hour," I said; "I must see Mr. Cressley immediately. Can you take me to his room?"

"If I am sure that you are Mr. John Bell," said the old man, glancing at me with not unnatural suspicion.

"Rest assured on that point. Here, this is my card, and here is a telegram which I received to-day from your master."

"But master sent no telegram to-day."

"You must be mistaken, this is from him."

"I don't understand it, sir, but you look honest, and I suppose I must trust you."

"You will do well to do so," I said.

He moved back and I entered the house. He took me down a passage, and then into a lofty chamber, which probably was the old banqueting-hall. As well as I could see by the light of the candle, it was floored, and panelled with black oak. Round the walls stood figures of knights in armour, with flags and banners hanging from the panels above. I followed the old man up a broad staircase and along endless corridors to a more distant part of the building. We turned now abruptly to our right, and soon began to ascend some turret stairs.

"In which room is your master?" I asked.

"This is his room, sir," said the man. He stood still and pointed to a door.

"Stay where you are; I may want you," I said.

I seized his candle, and holding it above my head, opened the door. The room was a large one, and when I entered was in total darkness. I fancied I heard a rustling in the distance, but could see no one. Then, as my eyes got accustomed to the faint light caused by the candle, I observed at the further end of the chamber a large four-poster bedstead. I immediately noticed something very curious about it. I turned round to the old housekeeper.

"Did you really say that Mr. Cressley was sleeping in this room?" I asked.

"Yes, sir; he must be in bed some hours ago. I left him in the library hunting up old papers, and he told me he was tired and was going to rest early."

"He is not in the bed," I said.

"Not in the bed, sir! Good God!" a note of horror came into the man's voice. "What in the name of fortune is the matter with the bed?"

As the man spoke I rushed forward. Was it really a bed at all? If it was, I had never seen a stranger one. Upon it, covering it from head to foot, was a thick mattress, from the sides of which tassels were hanging. There was no human being lying on the mattress, nor was it made up with sheets and blankets like an ordinary bed. I glanced above me. The posts at the four corners of the bedstead stood like masts. I saw at once what had happened. The canopy had descended upon the bed. Was Cressley beneath? With a shout I desired the old man to come forward, and between us we seized the mattress, and exerting all our force, tried to drag it from the bed. In a moment I saw it was fixed by cords that held it tightly in its place. Whipping out my knife, I severed these, and then hurled the heavy weight from the bed. Beneath lay Cressley, still as death. I put my hand on his heart and uttered a thankful exclamation. It was still beating. I was in time; I had saved him. After all, nothing else mattered during that supreme moment of thankfulness. A few seconds longer beneath that smothering mass and he would have been dead. By what a strange sequence of events had I come to his side just in the nick of time!

"We must take him from this room before he recovers consciousness," I said to the old man, who was surprised and horror-stricken.

"But, sir, in the name of Heaven, what has happened?"

"Let us examine the bed, and I will tell you," I said. I held up the candle as I spoke. A glance at the posts was all-sufficient to show me how the deed had been done. The canopy above, on which the heavy mattress had been placed, was held in position by strong cords which ran through pulleys at the top of the posts. These were thick and heavy enough to withstand the strain. When the cords were released, the canopy, with its heavy weight, must quickly descend upon the unfortunate sleeper, who would be smothered beneath it in a few seconds. Who had planned and executed this murderous device?

There was not a soul to be seen.

"We will take Mr. Cressley into another room and then come back," I said to the housekeeper. "Is there one where we can place him?"

"Yes, sir," was the instant reply; "there's a room on the next floor which was got ready for you."

"Capital," I answered; "we will convey him there at once."

We did so, and after using some restoratives, he came to himself. When he saw me he gazed at me with an expression of horror on his face.

"Am I alive, or is it a dream?" he said.

"You are alive, but you have had a narrow escape of your life," I answered. I then told him how I had found him.

He sat up as I began to speak, and as I continued my narrative his eyes dilated with an expression of terror which I have seldom seen equalled.

"You do not know what I have lived through," he said at last. "I only wonder I retain my reason. Oh, that awful room! no wonder men died and went mad there!"

"Well, speak, Cressley; I am all attention," I said; "you will be the better when you have unburdened yourself."

"I can tell you what happened in a few words," he answered. "You know I mentioned the horrid sort of presentiment I had about coming here at all. That first night I could not make up my mind to sleep in the house, so I went to the little inn at Brent. I received your telegram yesterday, and went to meet you by the last train. When you did not come, I had a tussle with myself; but I could think of no decent excuse for deserting the old place, and so came back. My intention was to sit up the greater part of the night arranging papers in the library. The days are long now, and I thought I might go to bed when morning broke. I was irresistibly sleepy, however, and went up to my room soon after one o'clock. I was determined to think of nothing unpleasant, and got quickly into bed, taking the precaution first to lock the door. I placed the key under my pillow, and, being very tired, soon fell into a heavy sleep. I awoke suddenly, after what seemed but a few minutes, to find the room dark, for the moon must just have set. I was very sleepy, and I wondered vaguely why I had awakened; and then suddenly, without warning, and without cause, a monstrous, unreasonable fear seized me. An indefinable intuition told me that I was not alone—that some horrible presence was near. I do not think the certainty of immediate death could have inspired me with a greater dread than that which suddenly came upon me. I dared not stir hand nor foot. My powers of reason and resistance were paralysed. At last, by an immense effort, I nerved myself to see the worst. Slowly, very slowly, I turned my head and opened my eyes. Against the tapestry at the further corner of the room, in the dark shadow, stood a figure. It stood out quite boldly, emanating from itself a curious light. I had no time to think of phosphorus. It never occurred to me that any trick was being played upon me. I felt certain that I was looking at my ancestor, Barrington Cressley, who had come back to torture me in order to make me give up possession. The figure was that of a man six feet high, and broad in proportion. The face was bent forward and turned toward me, but in the uncertain light I could neither see the features nor the expression. The figure stood as still as a statue, and was evidently watching me. At the end of a moment, which seemed to me an eternity, it began to move, and, with a slow and silent step, approached me. I lay perfectly still, every muscle braced, and watched the figure between half closed eyelids. It was now within a foot or two of me, and I could distinctly see the face. What was my horror to observe that it wore the features of my agent Murdock.

"'Murdock!' I cried, the word coming in a strangled sound from my throat. The next instant he had sprung upon me. I heard a noise of something rattling above, and saw a huge shadow descending upon me. I did not know what it was, and I felt certain that I was being murdered. The next moment all was lost in unconsciousness. Bell, how queer you look! Was it—was it Murdock? But it could not have been; he was very ill in bed at Liverpool. What in the name of goodness was the awful horror through which I had lived?"

"I can assure you on one point," I answered; "it was no ghost. And as to Murdock, it is more than likely that you did see him."

I then told the poor fellow what I had discovered with regard to the agent, and also my firm conviction that Wickham was at the bottom of it.

Cressley's astonishment was beyond bounds, and I saw at first that he scarcely believed me; but when I said that it was my intention to search the house, he accompanied me.

We both, followed by Mitchell, returned to the ill-fated room; but, though we examined the tapestry and panelling, we could not find the secret means by which the villain had obtained access to the chamber.

"The carriage which brought me here is still waiting just outside the lodge gates," I said. "What do you say to leaving this place at once, and returning, at least, as far as Carlton? We might spend the remainder of the night there, and take the very first train to Liverpool."

"Anything to get away," said Cressley. "I do not feel that I can ever come back to Cressley Hall again."

"You feel that now, but by-and-by your sensations will be different," I answered. As I spoke I called Mitchell to me. I desired him to go at once to the lodge gates and ask the driver of the wagonette to come down to the Hall.

This was done, and half an hour afterwards Cressley and I were on our way back to Carlton. Early the next morning we went to Liverpool. There we visited the police, and I asked to have a warrant taken out for the apprehension of Murdock.

The superintendent, on hearing my tale, suggested that we should go at once to Murdock's house in Melville Gardens. We did so, but it was empty, Murdock, his wife, and Wickham having thought it best to decamp. The superintendent insisted, however, on having the house searched, and in a dark closet at the top we came upon a most extraordinary contrivance. This was no less than an exact representation of the agent's head and neck in wax. In it was a wonderfully skilful imitation of a human larynx, which, by a cunning mechanism of clockwork, could be made exactly to simulate the breathing and low moaning of a human being. This the man had, of course, utilized with the connivance of his wife and Wickham in order to prove an alibi, and the deception was so complete that only my own irresistible curiosity could have enabled me to discover the secret. That night the police were fortunate enough to capture both Murdock and Wickham in a Liverpool slum. Seeing that all was up, the villains made complete confession, and the whole of the black plot was revealed. It appeared that two adventurers, the worst form of scoundrels, knew of Cressley's great discovery in Western Australia, and had made up their minds to forestall him in his claim. One of these men had come some months ago to England, and while in Liverpool had made the acquaintance of Murdock. The other man, Wickham, accompanied Cressley on the voyage in order to keep him in view, and worm as many secrets as possible from him. When Cressley spoke of his superstition with regard to the turret room, it immediately occurred to Wickham to utilize the room for his destruction. Murdock proved a ready tool in the hands of the rogues. They offered him an enormous bribe. And then the three between them evolved the intricate and subtle details of the crime. It was arranged that Murdock was to commit the ghastly deed, and for this purpose he was sent down quietly to Brent disguised as a journeyman the day before Cressley went to the Hall. The men had thought that Cressley would prove an easy prey, but they distrusted me from the first. Their relief was great when they discovered that I could not accompany Cressley to the Hall. And had he spent the first night there, the murder would have been committed; but his nervous terrors inducing him to spend the night at Brent foiled this attempt. Seeing that I was returning to Liverpool, the men now thought that they would use me for their own devices, and made up their minds to decoy me into Murdock's bedroom in order that I might see the wax figure, their object, of course, being that I should be forced to prove an alibi in case Murdock was suspected of the crime. The telegram which reached me at Prince's Hotel on my return from London was sent by one of the ruffians, who was lying in ambush at Brent. When I left Murdock's house, the wife informed Wickham that she thought from my manner I suspected something. He had already taken steps to induce the cab-driver to take me in a wrong direction, in order that I should miss my train, and it was not until he visited the stables outside the Prince's Hotel that he found that I intended to go by road. He then played his last card, when he telegraphed to the inn at Carlton to stop the horses. By Murdock's means Wickham and his confederate had the run of the rooms at the Hall ever since the arrival of Wickham from Australia, and they had rigged up the top of the old bedstead in the way I have described. There was, needless to say, a secret passage at the back of the tapestry, which was so cunningly hidden in the panelling as to baffle all ordinary means of discovery.

Printed in Great Britain
by Amazon

56397733R00081